★★★ THE ★★★
DURATION

A Novel of World War II San Francisco

By Richard Taylor

MaxM
LTD

THE DURATION

ISBN 978-0-9825132-1-7

First Printing

Cover illustration by Joe Phillips.
Book designed by David Maxine.

MaxM LTD.

[EDITOR'S NOTE]

Taylor uses some obscure words, so for the convenience of the reader, these are defined in endnotes. There are no obtrusive superscript numbers or footnotes, but if an unusual word is encountered, turn to the endnotes: next to the page number is the word or phrase and its explanation. Don't be intimidated, there aren't that many of them and you may learn a new term or two. Each term is only defined once, so if appears again in the book, the explanation will only be found under the page number on which it first appears.

The Duration is set on a fictional newspaper, *The Observer*, in San Francisco during World War II. When Mark Hanson was cleaning out his mother's things after her death, he found the manuscript—Taylor was married to Hanson's mother. Hanson had previously read another unpublished novel by Taylor, one set during the Civil War, (the whereabouts of that manuscript are known) and knew what a talented writer Taylor was. He eagerly read this manuscript which had not seen the light of day in almost half a century. Apparently Taylor had only sent the book out to one publisher—an unsolicited approach to Charles Scribner & Sons in 1964—and it was sent back. It sat unopened in a box, still in the brown paper wrapper in which it had been returned.

Richard Taylor had spent his entire working life in newspapers. After Hanson found the manuscript, he asked me to take a look at it as a friend, colleague and a professional writer. The manuscript is an interesting look at life for a 4-F reporter during World War II and life at newspapers in the 1940s—a life Taylor lived. However, when I asked Hanson if the main character's ways as a ladies' man were likely based on Taylor's own youth, he responded, "Oh, hell, no!" He was sure the novel was much more based in fantasy than in reality.

The manuscript is striking for how few errors it had in the typed pages. The writer in me wonders if he was typing from a hand-written manuscript or writing on the fly and getting it right the first time? Did he retype the pages until they were almost flawless, or was he that good a typist? I made only very minor edits.

The book is fascinating for its glimpse of that era, and even more so for what Richard Taylor's writing says about the education of learned men of that time. (And I do say men, because women were so rarely given the opportunity back then.) We chose to include the glossary at the end to spare the reader reaching for a dictionary or googling the obscure literary and historical references Taylor makes: Mayor Jimmy Rolph, Andromeda and Persues, the Bourbons, Charles V, Douglas Fairbanks, the Macedonians, Front de Boeuf, and many others (these are just in the first two chapters). The references provide insight as to how well-read newspapermen were in that time. Although the

The Duration

book is not a comedy, at times it put in mind of early
Dennis Miller, before he jumped the shark, when he
used to drop clever similes from antiquity like Henry II
dropped illegitimate progeny. The highly styled prose
put me in mind of some of the other great writers of the
World War II generation, such as Gore Vidal.

Taylor includes so much minutia about ration cards
and cable cars that it makes that time and place come
back to life. His description of the hard-drinking, have-
to-find-a-bar newspapermen made it clear that wives
and girlfriends were secondary to the next martini. The
attitude toward woman, like the attitude toward cigarettes — everyone smoked and cigarettes were so much a
part of every conversation — seems antiquated now. I
also found the name of the main character, who is
actively engaging in an extramarital affair prescient and
amusing: John Edwards. Some of the descriptions of
women and ethnic stereotypes seem very dated and
borderline offensive now.

For anyone who works in journalism today, it is a
fun look at how newspapers used to function when men
in green visors worked copy desks, bylines were given
sparingly, and smudges from carbon paper were a mark
of the trade. Enjoy the only known extant novel of
Richard Taylor.

Walter G. Meyer
Editor, MaxM Ltd.

[ONE]

Legend said the room hadn't been cleaned since 1906, when the building was rebuilt after the Fire; it was now 1943. The occupants' only sight of the exterior world was through three small windows at the rear which overlooked an alley, usually jammed with huge circulation trucks, their drivers lounging against the truck cabs and smoking, insouciant as mahouts. At dusk sweating and resentful copyboys struggled to seal these windows with heavy black tarpaulins; if a gleam of light escaped it might bring a Japanese bomb crashing down upon the city, or so everyone had believed fifteen months ago. These days, if a corner of a tarpaulin sagged free from a window in the course of the night, as usually happened, no one paid any attention. Maintaining the blackout had ceased to be interesting even as a means of keeping the copyboys up to the mark.

The light, day or night, came from globes hanging from the ceiling on long cords, their glare not much reduced by circular shades of exactly the tone of green which custom assigns to editors' eyeshades. (The night editor did wear one of those eyeshades, but he was the youngest man on the desk, and may have felt a need to affirm himself as an upholder and custodian of tradition.) From the lamps' sockets in turn hung long strings, ending about seven feet above the floor, which were yanked to turn on the lights. Each string was decorated at its end by a pierced playing card, usually an ace or deuce, a piece of picturesqueness which was ritually cherished: cards that weathered and fell off were replaced by an elder of the place, such as the bearded and pince-nez'd rim man who wrote his heads with a fountain pen, seldom hesitating, never striking out a word, though the *Observer* hadn't yet yielded to the new style of ragged heads, and still required headlines which counted exactly.

The desks — to imagine them new was a feat of the mind, like fleshing out one of those old, old Indian women into a pretty young maiden. New occupants looked into their desk drawers and were defeated immediately by sheer mass. They found: a report on imports and exports passing through the port of San Francisco in 1927; two grandstand press passes to the track at Tanforan, fall racing season, 1936; the agenda of the Planning Commission of the City and County of San Francisco for October 15, 1940; two Chinese lottery tickets; an Office of Price Administration directive, 52 pages, on the prices permissible to charge for dried raisins; a telephone number, written on a yellowed scrap of paper, which no one now remembered was the unlisted home number of Jimmy Rolph, the city's mayor for twenty years, later governor, now dead eleven years; hundreds of photo negatives, all unidentified.

The Duration

New reporters usually scooped a small hole in the desks' right-hand top drawer, like arrowhead makers settling into the tumuli left by former cultures; after that was filled, notes and press releases piled up on desk spikes. The view from the city desk ranged over an accumulation of moribund paper not often seen even in a newspapers' city room.

One Sunday morning when Edwards was the lone reporter working the early shift, beginning at nine o'clock, Frank Lemmon was the man on the desk. A huge, shambling, rather brooding man, Irish like everyone on the desk, Lemmon was assistant day city editor and wanted to go back to being a rewrite man, which he'd been before wartime drains on manpower forced him into his present chair. He hated the desk, the constant demands of the phones, the necessity of being disagreeable to reporters and the necessity of being suave or curt to the callers on the inexorable phones. Maybe once in two months, with great relish, he would smash a phone against the wall.

Early in the day, if it was quiet, he might write or rewrite a story himself, but not at his typewriter at the city desk; he walked out from behind the long desks with their battery of phones at which the city editors worked, and sat down at one of the cluster of three desks, just in front of the city desk, occupied by the rewrite men when they came in, around eleven. Hunched maternally or maybe vulpinely over the typewriter, caressing it with his beer belly, he wrote his story, sometimes talking a phrase to himself, hitting the keys delicately and very fast.

On this famous Sunday Lemmon had come in at nine-ten. Hung over, he contemplated the room. The telephones lay in their cradles like repressions accumulating intensity: they would take their toll later on. Calls at this hour, even on weekdays, were likely to be private: a wife with something that had slipped her mind, a lover wanting to say good morning, a creditor: people flexing the muscles of their rights, in the face of the sacredness of the working day.

"Let's get rid of some of this junk," Lemmon said to Edwards. He struck a match and set fire to a spiked pile of papers. It burned well; the fire spread to another spike; the fiery cleansing of 1906 appeared about to be repeated, Edwards beat at the flames with a copy of the thick Sunday edition. Lemmon swept one burning heap to the floor, where he kicked in a disgusted way. Copygirls ran to the powder room for water, which they brought in paper cups. When the fires were out Lemmon picked up the charred mass of paper he had knocked to the floor and set it down on a reporter's desk. He went behind his own desk, sat down and began to read the comics.

The typewriters were those old upright Underwoods, which newspapermen either swear by or hate. Cottontails frequently swung from the coats of staff members leaving on a story or to go home. The artists who retouched photographs or drew cartoons and diagrams to illustrate stories and did other small chores for the editorial department sat in an enclave at the back of the city room, by the windows that looked out on the alley. They were not kept very busy even in normal times; with newsprint rationed and the news being printed in seven-point type to save space and war-enriched advertisers claiming use of every inch and every line of the paper that postal regulations would allow, there wasn't much demand for the adornments the artists supplied, (though one of them had a god-like moment when the managing editor, convinced that General Eisenhower wasn't pushing forward as fast as he should in the invasion of North Africa, but feeling that an Associated Press map of the battlefront didn't establish his point, had a retoucher paint out the Atlas Mountains and move them twenty-five miles closer to the sea, to make the general look as if he were doing worse than he was). With the artists sat photographers between assignments. This group, not subject to the tensions that gripped the rest of the room and with only one telephone to ring among them, viewed their fellow workers as a spectacle, which they were perfectly willing to heighten.

They spent a good deal of their time putting together tails made of sticky tape and balls of cotton, which they fastened to the coattails of departing men preoccupied with the story they were going out on or the idea of the day's work being over. The city editor, Jimmy McKeon, whose blood may not have run with ink but whose lymph certainly contained caution, brushed incessantly with one hand behind him as he left each evening. Nevertheless they nailed him one night. Shrieks followed him down the corridor, but he was letting a conversation he'd had with the managing editor, concerning a name spelling three ways in one story, work on his incipient ulcers, and in his mournfulness he felt so cut off from all mankind that it never occurred to him that they were laughing at him.

A shipyard worker who stood next to him on the bus he rode home told him about the tail. "Lots of jokers where I work, too," the man said.

"Yeah, I heard," McKeon said, but he spoke gently: he was another who was a rewrite man at heart, and he thought he had done his quota for the day of bruising and scalding, not to mention having the same done to him.

Edwards, who was twenty-seven, had worked for the *Observer* three years, after a year on a suburban newspaper down the Peninsula, and eighteen months editing a house organ for a paint company. Desk men quickly learn the physical characteristics of a reporter's copy — how evenly or how raggedly he types, how hard he hits the keys and how long he is willing to put up with a frayed ribbon, how wide he makes his margins and how deeply he indents his paragraphs, what typographical mistakes he habitually makes — so well that often they can tell who wrote a story without glancing at the name in the upper left-hand corner of the copy.

They noted that Edward's copy gave an impression of spareness, neatness and competence; as for his style, it lacked dash or high polish. His typing was slightly rough, a characteristic a desk man might think significant; smooth typists tend to be either writers by rote, who never stop to let the right word catch up with them, or else the affianced, who stare around, hopeful that a phrase will manifest itself, and, if it makes itself known, type it out in one long and loving stroking of the keyboard. If the night rewrite man were to leave or to get tired of working five nights a week until two AM, Edwards probably would be the reporter chosen to replace him; the job called for a good steady man who could handle any sort of story, since after eleven PM he and Jack Cunningham, the night editor, would be alone in the office, and for a man who wrote reasonably well but not so well that he'd be a major loss to the day side. The present night rewrite man was an Irish Catholic who, no older than Edwards, had four children and financial problems, and was better off on all counts spending his nights working.

If he did quit, and Jimmy McKeon and Cunningham had a talk about replacing him with Edwards, one of the desk men would be sure to say to the other; but would he want to work nights? It wasn't just that

The Duration

Edwards was a bachelor. It was a matter of his origins, which by now almost had been forgiven him, but occasionally were remembered. His father was a lawyer, a partner in a firm well thought of along Montgomery Street. His mother's name meant a good deal in the cubicle from which the women's pages were edited — her mother was from one of those Spanish California families, which live in the inmost of the Chinese puzzle boxes of San Francisco society: you almost never see their names in the women's pages; they prefer to keep their eminence gray; their very existence often is unknown to the socially ambitious wives of pediatricians and dentists.

Edwards had gotten the job on his own, but he had been at work only a few days when the publisher — a bland Jewish gentleman among all those feisty Irishmen; a satrap in the publishing empire in which the *Observer* had been the first province — came into the city room for a brief talk with the city editor, after which he looked around quite deliberately until he found Edwards, came over to Edwards' desk and asked him how he was getting on, and left observing over his shoulder, "I saw your father at lunch the other day."

All this was observed from the city desk with a malice originally nurtured on a diet of potatoes, or not enough potatoes. Some word must have been passed, late at night in Malloy's bar or the Press Club or maybe it was just that a tribal unease had been stirred, without anything being said; two days later Edwards, who had been out of college three years at the time, was asked what college he'd gone to, by a photographer who glanced from Edwards' tweed sports jacket to his cordovans. Edwards was not happy. He bought two muted and under-priced suits. As he stood before the city desk, distributing his copy — the original into the copy

[7]

basket, the pieces of carbon paper into another basket, the three dupes onto spikes, one for the desk's reference, one for the AP, one for good luck—the desk men eyed his suit: you have a new suit, they commented silently.

All Edwards could do was wait for the suits to age into some approximation of the almost ostentatiously drab clothes the desk men wore. (An interesting variation on this theme of inconspicuous consumption had been worked out by Cunningham, who wore suits or a suit, of clerical darkness and cut, and a black felt hat, also priestly; give him a round collar and above it you'd instantly have recognized the bold, blunt, bellicose features of one hot-spoken sort of Irish priest.)

Over this busy, grimy, tattered room a presence brooded, haunting it pretty much in the same way the Good Duke's wraith had presided over Nepenthe. Nose after ears, the Good Duke had said cheerfully when he was alive, warning his subjects of the penalties of disaffection the Chief, who though unseen was still alive and reigning over his twenty-two newspapers (if at the moment as a constitutional monarch whose whims were subject to veto by his banker) always had favored Assyrian methods. A murmur of discontent of unrest reached him, and five highly-placed heads and five ordinary ones rolled: in some cases their owners' offense would have been only to reveal too conscious a sense of their own value to the *Observer*. The shocked survivors, as they say in old histories, were docile and unresisting. Nowadays, though, his teeth had been drawn (literally, too).

Good men, or men of any kind, were in short supply as a result of the war, so decimation was out. Besides, he had piled the mistakes of Louis XV on the mistakes of Louis XIV—expenditure like a hemorrhage, a mistress who made him vulnerable to satire, Bourbon pigheadedness; the Pyrenees had survived, despite him, and grown into Himalayas; the deluge hadn't waited; he had thrown himself onto the marble mercies of banks, who had taken away his pen and checkbook, put him on an annual personal dole which was the equivalent of what once he had spent every two days, and sternly lopped off, by sale, merger or simple extinction, his unprofitable newspaper properties. The operation had been a success, but something in the patient must have died. His mistress, who was no brighter than Marie Antoinette but had learned when young what cake cost, sold her jewels to help tide him over they closed down the great seaside palaces in which they had frolicked, and retreated to his huge lodge in the Sierra, a wooden palace like Attila's — no one ever has been able to think of him except in terms of imperial or royal personages, and in a way he was the heir to all those monarchs: their treasures filled his own Sans Soucis; he even had something of Attila's, a method or two he had borrowed.

After moving to the Sierra he stayed in seclusion; he was not heard from very much. Occasionally an exhortation — in favor of accuracy and hard-hittingness and other standard virtues — appeared on the bulletin board in the *Observer's* city room, partly written in the capitals, which he used lavishly in editorials. Other messages, suggesting that the imperial prerogative hadn't lapsed altogether, sometimes were received. One evening a reporter was sent out to scour the city for Armenian grape leaves, wanted for a dinner to be given in the mountains next night. The cooking of the Levant wasn't well-known then; and the man given this mission had, thanks to some bungling in the transmission of his orders, less idea than the dove that Noah loosed

[9]

over the Middle East that he was intended to bring back a leaf. He wasted a good deal of time looking for Armenian grapes.

Secluded and resting from the burdens of state the Chief might be — to that extent the monarch he resembled at the moment was Charles V (who had relaxed by rehearsing his own funeral, with himself in the coffin); but whatever he was practicing up there in the Sierra, it wasn't his own rites. His horror and distaste at the idea of his own dissolution were famous. His obituary not only wasn't written in any part; the materials for it weren't kept in the *Observer's* library, with all other clippings and files of news matter, but were in the personal files of the Observer's publisher, in an envelope carefully marked "Materials for Biography of Chief," to forestall anything being made of it by anybody nosing around.

Sometimes a reporter and photographer would be sent to the mountain retreat, to record some distinction being conferred on the Chief by the American Legion or the DAR. His likeness always was ordered retouched, but the photographers — rather meanly, since everyone dispatched on these assignments testified to being treated exactly as he treated all his guests, with eccentric courtesy and bountiful hospitality — always made unretouched prints, which were passed around the office so everyone could admire the job time was doing on him.

Although he was barely eighty he had enough wrinkles you could imagine him boasting of having started the Civil War instead of that other one. These days he was not only visibly mortal, and sat in the mountains cabin'd, cribbed and confined by bankers, but also was pleasingly subject to the wartime annoyances which afflicted everybody. One night the city desk received an urgent telephone call from the mountains. A special delivery letter was to follow. It contained the Chief's shoe ration stamps, which were about to expire; somebody tomorrow was to go out and buy him a pair, specifications for which would be enclosed.

*   *   *   *   *

The only hat on the hat tree, at five-thirty on this winter evening, was Cunningham's black one. The hat tree stood by the city desk. All the desk men wore hats; on the lower levels of the staff, only some of the older men did. It was a pleasant time of day. The deadline of the first edition was an hour past. This edition, already on the streets, contained most of the local news that would be in tomorrow's paper — barring murder, fire, the outbreak of scandal, or something developed from one of those notes on potential stories (always typed entirely in lower case, which was part of the tradition) that Jimmy McKeon would leave for Cunningham.

Only a skeleton staff would work until eleven, after which there would remain just Cunningham and the night rewrite man, who between eleven and midnight, the early hour at which the bars closed by fiat of the Army, would take turns going downstairs to Malloy's bar. The late shift reporters, who had come in at one or two p.m., by five-thirty still hadn't entirely lost a relaxed air of having spent the morning mowing their lawns or of having been up to no good, according to their temperaments. The early shift reporters, leaving at five-thirty, had a relaxed air of heading for their homes or Malloy's, according to their temperaments.

By five-thirty Frank Lemmon had taken his hat and left, looking like a bear wearing a hat. Jimmy McKeon had taken his hat (which was as black as Cunningham's, but jauntier, somewhere between the

[11]

priestly style and Douglas Fairbanks, Jr.) and left, looking as sad and tired as if he were fifty-three; he was just past thirty. The phones on Jimmy's desk (at which Cunningham now sat) bit into McKeon's back if they rang as he was rounding the hat tree and heading for the door through which he would escape. Sometimes he waited to see if Cunningham would call him back; sometimes he simply plunged on. Cunningham had the first edition spread out flat on his desk and was turning over the pages, looking for errors, which he greatly enjoyed finding. His face reflected, a mixture of the slight jealousy every newspaperman feels at seeing an edition of his paper that has been put out without his help, and a mild skepticism that it could have been done well.

The quality of the light, from the bulbs hanging overhead changed at this hour. Its harshness wasn't so apparent in the busy hours of the afternoon, when the room was full of movement and people. Now it dropped on the few men in the room as bleakly as the light in some institutional building—a police station, maybe. Cunningham was the desk sergeant; clearly there was no Irish role he wasn't competent to portray.

Outside was the city. Its pulse, at five o'clock, runs fast; it sets itself to seduce its inhabitants; promise then anything, is its motto. At five o'clock, in the hurry of the brisk, darkening, formal, geometric streets, it is impossible not to feel that the evening does hold promise— has made you a promise the haste and hopefulness of the people on the streets are given tinge and tone by girls; beginning at four-thirty, the buildings of the financial district pour out their true wealth—a Fort Knox's hoard of healthy, handsome, high-stepping girls.

Five nights a week, in every season, they communicate to the air a case of spring fever. Its symptoms could

The Duration

be felt even in this crypt, where the aging copyreaders sat in a circle, resigned and dusty as the memories of once-potent kings.

Edwards was ready to go. He tipped his typewriter forward so that it disappeared into the desk. He hid two copy pencils and an eraser in the back of a drawer, where they probably would be safe. To open the drawer of another man's desk and scoop out a pencil casually, with the air of meaning to put it back after using it for an instant, was one thing; but to burrow in the recesses of a confrere's desk took gall or an unusual degree of fury at the parsimony of management.

Passing Cunningham's desk, Edwards said goodnight. Cunningham just had found something in the paper which he had circled with a pounce of pencil. There was a slight delay then he said, "Goodnight, John." It was nice of him to have spoken; he'd had to drop the mouse from his jaws. Edwards took the elevator down to the lobby, walked through a cigar store hung with racing forms and tip sheets, and out on to Market Street. It was meant to be a splendid street. It is broad; it cuts diagonally through the city's cross-hatch of streets like Alexander's sword through the knot, creating fantastic traffic patterns that remind you Alexander had a heritage of lunacy, its character had been coarsening for years, but the extent of its decline became apparent only with the onset of the war, when it began to permit familiar ties to sailors—even welcomed them. Shooting galleries and tattoo parlors blossomed. Credit jewelers flourished. It became a kind of Panama Canal Zone, lying athwart the city, resented and disparaged by the natives. It had always had the quality of a dangerous jungle corridor—streetcars charged down it four abreast, nose to tail, like elephants in must, shrilling rage as the motormen, indulging their nerves at the expense of everybody else's, stamped on their warning bells.

The *Observer* Building was on the south side of Market; behind it lay flophouses, Skid Road, Skid Road bars. Beyond the north side of the street were the city's delights, Edwards tonight wasn't pleasure-bound — not exactly. He wasn't going home, either. He lived in one of those ramshackle frame apartment houses on Russian Hill, with a view like an archangel's. His apartment was on the ground floor, in concession to his heart, which seemed sound enough these days, but had been battered about by rheumatic fever when he was a child. Even on the ground floor, he paid a high rent, (he had a small life income, left him by his grandmother, which permitted him some luxuries).

Once he had brought a rich girl from Kansas City home with him. Next morning, she looked with horror at the sleazy, perilous flight of fifty wooden stairs, which led down the hill to the next apartment building. Naturally she didn't care for heights, but it was plain this slapdash staircase implied to her an unforgivably casual attitude toward altitude. If the word brinkmanship had been invented then, she would have felt: this is poor man's brinkmanship. Edwards guessed then, and learned later, she thought she had spent a night in the slums.

When Edwards was going home, he walked up Market to O'Farrell, and took the O'Farrell, Jones and Hyde cable car most evenings, though, he did as he did this night: he walked to Powell and took the Washington and Jackson car.

[TWO]

The gripman threw himself backward and tugged at the cable car's big brake, standing two-thirds as tall as he did, Edwards, who was light on his feet, dropped from the step while the car was still in motion; the gripman, taking his cue like a figure in ballet, already was releasing the brake as Edwards leaped, and the car hardly lost way at all. With a pleasing sense of having propelled a whole carload of passengers on their way Edwards started up the hill toward Margaret's apartment.

Two girls in shipyard worker's tin hats and bulky work clothes climbed the hill ahead of him. He passed dingy apartment houses, each with a "no vacancy" sign on the door; some of the signs originally had said the contrary, and had been converted by a "NO" written in at the top with fierce relish.

Two blocks below the building where Margaret lived he stopped in at a corner liquor store. A man he didn't know was buying something, so Edwards stared at the shelves where a few bottles of whiskey, survivors of better days, were jostled about by a crowd of rum bottles and Old Southern liquors. When the man Edwards didn't recognize had gone out Edwards went over to the cash register and asked the store's owner for cigarettes. The storekeeper was a large loud swaggering man who seemed as out of place in this neighborhood business as Long John would have been in his galley if Silver had been a loudmouth, but he must have had a different view of the matter, since he was in the store sixteen hours a day, six days a week. He reached beneath the counter and came up with two packs of a second-rate brand. Now and then he let loose a pack of Camels or Chesterfields. Edwards took what he was offered without comment, since it was 1943. He climbed on toward Margaret's.

The street, which had been steep, became precipitous; the last block before Edwards' lovers' abode was enough to make anybody puff, but Edwards didn't, partly because he walked slowly, sparing himself, and partly because, like many newspapermen, he was lean, though he wasn't one of the coughing unhealthy Irish ones, nor one of the restless quivering ones with long straight noses whose resemblance to bird dogs long ago became so widely noted that it congealed into a standard perception.

He was a neat spare man, not very tall — a little over five feet seven, or five feet eight if you wanted to accept the official statistic he gave out. His hair was blond and carefully brushed with a pair of military brushes. He had confident blue eyes and a ruddy face. If you had blown him up with a bicycle pump he would have been formidable, one of those Front de Boeuf types who turn out to be fourth generation millionaires besides. Since he worked for his living, and was the size that he was, most people liked him.

The Duration

Margaret couldn't put a light in her window to let him know that she was home, because of the blackout. They had arranged that when she arrived home she would black out her bedroom window, even if it was still light outside; if she wasn't home the shade in her bedroom would be pulled halfway down. Of course Edwards had a key, which he used if he came by later at night, after working late; but he and Margaret had agreed, felicitating one another on their common sense in a slightly formal, slightly touchy manner: rather like a married couple reaching concord on what agreeable luxuries it's necessary to cut from their household budget—that it wouldn't do for him, around six o'clock when other tenants in the apartment house were coming home too, to be seen letting himself in with his own key.

It was true the other tenants saw him arriving home with Margaret, nearly every evening; but it was a tolerant city at any time, and in this time of war and trouble most people were too busy or anxious, or too involved in something of their own that wouldn't stand full daylight, to mind the business of others. Anyway, there was a feeling current that morals or at least moralizing, were somehow unpatriotic: censuring other people's conduct was a luxury, and so it was out for the duration.

Edwards might be a combat veteran, just discharged, who had suffered terrible nervous or physical damage on Guadalcanal, for which he was seeking to console himself with Margaret or he might be due to join the Army or Navy in the next thirty days specifically for some desperate mission from which he was unlikely to return. How could you know? Better not to meddle and be snubbed, or looked at as if you were suspected of spying. (Edwards was 4-F.)

The Duration

But his own key, openly displayed, would have been a different matter. It might have put the building's owner, a clubwomanly widow who lived in the first apartment off the lobby as you came in from the front door, in a position where she might have felt that propriety wouldn't permit her to look the other way.

Edwards and Margaret tried to preserve appearances. He usually left her between five and six in the morning. This was riskier than it sounds, since shipyards and war plants were working around the clock, and people came and went at all hours; actually, he was safer on the mornings when he was working a late shift at the paper, and slept in until around nine-thirty. He avoided the elevator, and used the stairs, on which he could wait if he heard voices in the hall of the floor below. The stairs didn't squeak, which was more than could be said for the springs on Margaret's bed. Margaret worried about this, in the small hours of the night, but he thought that sometimes she took a fierce defiant joy in the sound they made.

The blind in Margaret's window was pulled halfway down, Edwards walked up the hill another block, to the top; from here the street slanted down to the bay. Between the apartment houses lining the street you could see only a slice of the bay, like light at the end of a tunnel; or really, since it was dark now, Edwards couldn't see the bay at all: only memory enabled him to discern where the water began. In peacetime the dark out there would have had known dimensions imposed on it by the Alcatraz lighthouse, its revolving beam sweeping across the sky; lower down, he might have seen the masthead lights of a ship hurrying into port, with that air of mystery and importance they took on at this hour—N. Bonaparte, passage booked at Elba, might be aboard, or Roger Casement.

The Duration

A few lights did show at windows down the street; people were getting careless about the blackout now. It wasn't like a year ago, in the spring of 1942, when his friends had been full of marvelously improbable theories of how the Japanese, come July and August, were going to bomb the city from aircraft carriers hidden in the fog banks which lie massively off the Golden Gate in the summer months. "We'll be bombed by July," pretty women said in bars, with all the authoritativeness conferred on them by Red Cross uniforms. Edwards turned around and walked down the hill toward Margaret's. He was not so sure nowadays that this loitering was better than brazening out the business of the key.

Sometimes, strolling around the block while waiting for Margaret, he met tenants going home to Margaret's building, whose slight smiles suggested recognition of the walk of a man who's killing time, not a man who's heading for home. But the conversation with Margaret concerning the key had been a difficult one and he didn't want to reopen it. He wanted to avoid discussions, wanted time for their relationship to take on body, until it seemed more normal and natural to her than her marriage, which, after all, had lasted only six months, so far as actually living with Harry was concerned. She had known Harry for three months before they were married, and was still married to him.

Margaret came up the hill. He recognized her first as a glimmer of white gloves, then as a spill of blonde hair. They sometimes were mistaken for brother and sister. Edwards didn't relish this, but deceived himself concerning the exact damage that was done to his pride: the real reason he disliked being thought Margaret's brother was that he secretly feared people thought him her brother because he was barely taller than she. He recognized it could be useful if the apartment house tenants thought them brother and sister, but he doubted that the tenants did. He wasn't above saying loudly in the hall, "Did you hear from mother today?", but this was mostly to amuse Margaret, who laughed hard at the idea of incest because she couldn't (most of the time) afford to find adultery funny.

Margaret was carrying a bag of groceries; she looked fresh and her step was springy. Sometimes she came home dragging. Her work, as a secretary in a law firm, wasn't really arduous, but she made it harder than it was and probably it was made harder for her. Except in the shipyards, where happy rustics from Arkansas and Oklahoma reveled incredulously in prosperity and wished only that every war could last a hundred years, civilian guilt sat heavily on the city. The Parkinson's Law of wartime was that work expanded in proportion to the need of the worker, or his chief, to feel that anything could be anywhere nearly as important as risking your life. Margaret placed and spaced her semi-colons as if they were sniper's bullets.

She smiled at Edwards, shifted the groceries to her left arm, tucked her right hand under his arm. "Goodies, darling," she said, "My nice little butcher had two lamb chops saved for me, and he wouldn't take any stamps."

Margaret was an earnest and an honest girl, but she felt that authority and all its works — such as food rationing — were masculine and at that, represented masculinity at its most vulnerable. She took a cool semi-erotic pleasure in flouting regulations. Furthermore, when she outwitted authority she wanted to let a man know what she was doing: it gave her a sense of permitting him a blinding glimpse of womanly realism and power, as if she had allowed a strange man to look down the front of her dress and then had moved away, dismissingly blowing cigarette smoke at him.

They walked up three shallow concrete stairs to the building's front door. This was always an awkward moment, when Margaret looked into her mailbox to see if there was a letter from Harry, in the South Pacific. Still holding onto Edwards, still holding on to the groceries, Margaret swung around in front of Edwards and dipped neatly to peer through the glass of her mailbox. Edwards thought she was overdoing it, he had seen from the sidewalk that a white shape showed through the glass, and he was sure that she had seen it too.

Margaret let go of Edwards' arm and began trying to find the mailbox key in her purse without putting down the groceries. Edwards watched her for a minute and then took the grocery bag from her; she smiled at him, widely and warmly, which gave him an odd embarrassed sensation, as if he had caught her in a lie. "Not enough damn hands," she mumbled, still poking in the purse.

Edwards would have sworn she had found the key by now, and was prolonging the search out of some feeling that to produce it too easily would argue eagerness to get her mail.

When at last she got the envelope out of the mailbox Margaret stood for a long moment looking at it. It appeared to be a bill. He didn't think she had a disappointed look, but she stood there in preoccupation, as if something had jolted her: perhaps it was her name, Mrs. Harry Reynolds, which he could see typed on the envelope. She had told him that in the brief span of her actual life with Harry her married name hadn't had time to become completely her own; she seemed to hint that shedding it wouldn't be too difficult. Perhaps she had expected a letter from Harry, and had been ready for it in a slightly hostile frame of mind for, though she was far from having decided against Harry and for Edwards, still Edwards was the here and now, and there may have seemed to her something importunate, something tactless about Harry's letters, waiting in the mailbox for her to come home with Edwards. In that mood, her married name, scrawled on an envelope in Harry's small nondescript hand, might seem to her a downright presumption, Harry taking too much for granted. It might be a shock then to see the name in formal typed characters, as if the world were standing up for Harry's rights.

Margaret put the envelope in her purse, unlocked the building's front door and they went silently into the lobby. They met no one on the way to Margaret's apartment. The apartment was small, shabby and incurably rusty, but Margaret was lucky to have it. The city, built on a peninsula's tip, even in peacetime had been a tight squeeze for its inhabitants, its houses built wall against wall and most people ant-hilling it in apartments and rooming houses, or small hotels (which existed here in greater numbers than in any other American city except New York and Chicago). In San Francisco in 1943 many war wives were living in single rooms, cooking off electric hot plates and using a communal bathroom; or sharing with three other girls an apartment no bigger than Margaret's. She had been lucky, too, in the way in which she'd secured it for herself alone. Before her it had been occupied by Jane Stennett, a Navy wife too, whom Margaret had met and traded small talk with during coffee breaks in the cafeteria of the building where they both worked.

Jane was a big, handsome, dark-haired, white-skinned girl with a confident manner. She shared her apartment with another girl. When the other girl moved out Jane asked Margaret if she'd like to move in. "The Navy takes care of its own," she said, a little morosely. Margaret had noticed that Jane seemed to be taking the war increasingly hard. Margaret, who was still living in the hotel room where she and Harry had stayed in the ten days before he sailed, (it was ridiculously expensive in proportion to her income, but she didn't know where else to go), jumped at the chance. (Margaret's mother, in San Diego, occasionally was on the phone wondering why Margaret didn't come home—it was mere bemusement on her part, she never would have suspected Margaret of straying in the slightest—but Margaret, though she loved her family, felt after Harry left that she had a great deal of sudden and recent experience to assimilate, and didn't want her family eavesdropping while she communed with herself.)

She and Jane fell into a comfortable pattern; half-somnolent in this time of waiting, they were as easy with one another as a couple of mothers waiting for their children to be born. They rode the cable car to work together; they encouraged one another to be bold and leave off the troublesome leg makeup, which they wore to work instead of their few precious pairs of stockings and just go to the office barelegged. They told one another, in a friendly but guarded way about their husbands, steering away instinctively from talk about sex; it was easier, lying in the dark, to talk about their fears than their deprivations. They talked a good deal about their college days, laughing about the hopeful and lustful boys with whom they'd gone out; blotting out the most recent chapter of their lives as women they firmly restored sex to its former slightly comic status.

They went out on double dates, with Navy officers they met at officers' club dances on Treasure Island; sometimes they allowed themselves to be picked up in bars, though there was an unwritten rule that this could happen only if the men were Navy officers. Coming home from these evenings, they giggled like college girls over the too obvious aspirations of the men who took them out. One night, when Jane and her date were riding in the back seat of the car which one of the men miraculously had summoned up from somewhere — it was the first time in nearly a year that either girl had gone out for the evening in a car, instead of a taxi or streetcar; that incredible man even had even come up with a "C" windshield sticker and ration book, entitling him to all the gasoline he wanted — Margaret became conscious that very heavy necking was taking place behind her.

That night there was no post mortem of the date. Next morning Margaret left for work before Jane; she slapped her gloves in a cavalier way against the door-frame of the bedroom, where Jane was still frowzing about as she left. Jane had a date with the same man that night, but not a double date; she came in very late. Margaret lay awake and asked herself if she could find the nerve to ask Jane: how does it feel to have a man in you who aren't your husband. But she failed to ask Jane this because she had to acknowledge the question would have sprung from curiosity as much as from the intent to rebuke.

Three days later Jane said she thought she'd rather wait out the war in the Ohio town she came from; she was going home to her parents. After she left Margaret did nothing about finding a roommate. She was content to be alone, and she could easily afford the rent, frozen at a low figure by the Office of Price Administration. Jane had been gone a few days when Margaret ran into Mrs. Arnold, the building's owner, in the lobby. Mrs. Arnold asked if Margaret were planning to have another girl share her apartment. Margaret recognized that the significance of this question was that the rent, though frozen, increased by $2.50 a month if two persons lived in the apartment. She told Mrs. Arnold she'd be glad to pay the full figure. To avoid any imputation of being unpatriotic or ungregarious, she added, untruthfully, "I'm expecting my husband home soon, on a long leave." (Well, who knew? Harry was on a carrier, he must know a lot of fliers. There were those stories about fliers on forty-eight hours leave at Pearl Harbor who persuaded somebody taking a transport plane back to the states on a quick turn-around to let them stow away, and turned up unexpectedly on their presumably delighted wives' doorsteps.) This fortunate remark must have made it easier, later, for Mrs. Arnold to take Edwards in her stride. Maybe Edwards was Margaret's husband. Who knew?

Margaret wrote Harry a letter saying that Jane had gone home to her family, and that she thought she'd rather live by herself for a while. She included an account of Jane's behavior and then took it out again, telling herself it might upset him. This was after Margaret had met Edwards. For some reason she carried the revised letter in her purse for several days without mailing it. She began thinking that she shouldn't mail this letter at all; she'd write another full of up-to-date news. The up-to-date letter didn't include any mention of Jane's leaving; there was no room in such a newsy letter for old news.

After mailing that letter she felt guilty (on account of not writing often) and wrote again in four days. Harry didn't get another letter for almost three weeks. It was a long one, full of news. The news it didn't contain was nothing Harry would have wanted to hear.

[THREE]

Margaret went into the small kitchen with the groceries. On her way she tossed her purse into a big shabby overstuffed chair. (Nearly everything in the apartment was run down or badly worn, but Margaret despised girls in her circumstances who determinedly tried to improve their wartime lodgings with good reproductions on the wall and driftwood and a spot of color here and there; her attitude was that she wasn't accepting any of it, the war or consumer good shortages or living as she did; she was living under protest; she kept the apartment free of dust and perfectly clean, and that was all.)

She would throw the purse into the chair with exactly the same gesture if it happened to contain an unopened, letter from Harry. But occasionally, as soon as they were in the apartment, she would say to Edwards in a formal voice, "Forgive me a moment, John," and open Harry's letter and read it. She read rapidly but not hastily, as if looking for information that was not especially welcome to her. Edwards couldn't tell from her expression, whether the information she needed was a matter of mere fact, or a report on somebody's feelings — Harry's or her feeling about what Harry felt.

As to the first supposition, Harry came from a mon-eyed family and had money of his own; though he was thirty-five hundred miles from his money and his wife, he probably could derive some relief from being able to say what should be done with his money, and an even greater comfort from being able to tell his wife what she should tell others to do with his money. To entrust Margaret with some responsibility for his money was to remind her of its existence, a reminder he must feel could do no harm; but more importantly, to entrust Margaret with his money was to reassure himself that his marriage really existed and still was in working order.

As to the second supposition: one evening when Margaret had read a letter from Harry she crammed it hastily, almost angrily into her bag and went straight to the kitchen, where she mixed strong drinks of that awful wartime bourbon for herself and Edwards. After she had drunk most of hers, talking a little about her day and asking Edwards about his, she took hold of both Edwards' hands and led him into her bedroom. That letter: had Harry, speaking of his longing, roused her pity to such heights that it encompassed her and Edwards as well as poor hard-up Harry? Or had he sim-ply stirred her sensuality by detailing past pleasures he hoped to enjoy again? Maybe, far within her, flickered a wicked wish to be taken while the picture of Harry's deprivation was still vivid before her.

Still, by whom that evening had Margaret been mounted? Edwards, thrusting into her, had thought of

Harry in the same action, and felt the thought reinforce his own thrust. Maybe Margaret was doing some mingling too; she may even have been deeply female enough to believe that, since she couldn't serve or be served by Harry, she was doing her best by allowing herself to be served by Harry's vicar. If she knew — and she probably could guess some of what was in Edwards' mind, if she guessed that his nerves tingled with Harry's impulses, couldn't she almost believe, even though her flesh assured her that it wasn't Harry cleaving her, that it was Harry she was bringing to release?

Tonight, glad for an evening without Harry lurking inside that purse, Edwards followed Margaret into the kitchen, with a sense of warmth and confidence, and watched her put away the groceries. She seemed, it crossed his mind, very occupied with this.

"How about a drink, John," she said, not looking at him. Her tone was strained; she sounded as if she were offering a drink to a man she didn't know very well who'd given her a ride home from work, and whom she'd be just as glad to see on his way.

Though she had laid the tiniest stress on a note of hospitality, he answered, "I'll do it," choosing to stand on his prerogative because he thought he knew what was coming next. He took the bottle from beneath the sink, and assertively removed ice trays from the refrigerator and ice from the trays.

As he handed her a drink Margaret came out with it. "There'll only be time for one, John," she said. "I have a date tonight."

He accepted this, sipping his drink. He couldn't live with Margaret not only because such a step always becomes known or is sensed, even on the other side of an ocean; not only because Harry might turn up, out of the blue; but because too many of the men going and coming from the war, friends of Harry's or men who had known Margaret in school or college, who were likely not only to telephone her unexpectedly that they were in town but also, in the spirit of the times, to show up without notice at her front door, confident of their welcome and carrying a bottle to cheer up the dull evenings of Harry's Margaret.

Edwards — who twice had been trapped by such visitors and had been explained away by Margaret as somebody who'd just dropped by for a drink before they went out for some nice safe entertainment such as a concert — thought that in spite of their bonhomie there was a certain vindictiveness in the manner in which some of these men descended on Margaret without warning.

It wasn't that they expected or hoped to catch her misbehaving; quite obviously, those who found him in her apartment were surprised and displeased, and on the other hand not ready to jump to conclusions. But these men, when younger, perhaps never had been able to spend an evening with pretty Margaret without calling her ten days before. It was their pleasure now to find her, they expected, as tied to her hearth and with as little freedom to maneuver as any Victorian girl; presumably she would be grateful for their attention, and even if she weren't she would be bound by the rules of the day — they were men about to be in great peril or men who just had been — to concede them an evening at least.

Men who'd hoped vainly to make free of her person could now get back at her a little by making a rape of her time, by demanding and receiving her company as if by right, sprawling in her big armchair, letting her bring them drinks from the bottle they kindly had provided.

The Duration

Edwards took another sip. "Friend of Harry's?" he asked.

"Friend of mine."

Sometimes it seemed to Edwards that he minded these old acquaintances more than he minded Harry. Harry had in Edwards' mind an air of inevitability; Edwards never had known Margaret without Harry in the background. Harry supplied most of the tension in their life together; remove Harry, and they might be in danger of finding one another dull, and perhaps occasionally would have to invoke Harry's memory as a stimulant. Sometimes he wondered what they ever would find to talk about as interesting as the problem of Harry.

"Let's hash it over some more," Margaret would say happily, her blonde hair falling over one eye as she took a deep swig of her drink. (Of course there were bleak times when she shuddered away from all mention of Harry, for her own sake or Edwards or both.) Suppose it were in Edwards' power to blot out Harry, retroactively, and wipe out Margaret's marriage to him, would he do so? The official view, which Edwards maintained even to himself, had to be that he would. But when he tried to picture that simpler Margaret, that virgin Margaret, that unencumbered Margaret, she took on for him the look of an early and uncompleted work, standing in archaic pose, her knees clamped firmly together.

If you postulated the inevitability of Harry, you had to concede the inevitability of Harry's friends. Margaret's pre-Harry men friends annoyed Edwards much more, because they so resolutely refused to admit that they were anachronisms. Harry's friends, except for the one who had found Edwards in Margaret's apartment, didn't know that Edwards so much as exist-

[30]

ed; but obviously Edwards could afford to be patronizing about them. (How many of Harry's friends, if they
knew Margaret was being unfaithful, would have a try
at making her themselves? How many did try, even as
it was?) But Margaret's old friends, if the one whom
Edwards had met by mischance in the apartment was
any sample, were determined to treat Harry as if he
were a mistake in taste that Margaret had made, and an
unimportant mistake at that. They talked to Margaret,
Edwards gathered, only about times and scenes before
Harry's appearance, early in the war, in San Diego,
where Margaret had grown up and was then living
with her parents.

Harry had been an ensign, temporarily assigned to
duty with the Eleventh Naval District. The manner and
timing of his capture of Margaret rankled with the
young men who had known Margaret for years and
hoped themselves to marry her, or at least to go off to
the wars with some memory to fondle—some would
have settled for a tender statement of regard, which in
the context of the time amounted to an emotional prom-
issory note with a cash-in value about that of
Confederate currency in early 1865; others hoped for
grosser concessions. (This had been in the spring of
1942, when most of Margaret's friends were training
somewhere, or were angling for a commission or to get
into any branch except the Army, or just waiting to be
drafted; only a couple of the boys she knew were actually overseas yet.)

Margaret was a Catholic, brought up in a household
whose Catholicism was tempered by the unspoken
reservations of her mother, a good-humored Yankee
from Vermont from whom Margaret had her coloring
and a habit of deflation that kept its teeth sharp on the
Irish enthusiasms she inherited from her father; every

day, sometimes in the span of a single sentence that began in a burst and ended lamely or wryly, she reenacted within herself her parent's marriage. She attended a convent school and a Jesuit College. By the time she was a college freshman she smoked, drank and necked with moderate abandon. In her senior year she came right to the brink of having an affair with a young Jesuit instructor — a possibility the men she dated dimly saw, and rejected as impossible; the Protestants were far more shocked than the Catholics. Margaret thought later that she might have gone to bed with the priest (she would have been the one who made the decision, at every level of decision) if it hadn't been that by that time she had lost her faith — otherwise the Irish side of her mightn't have been able to resist the sinfulness and mystery of It. There were still times when she wondered, she told Edwards.

"When you wonder what?"

"Oh, John, sometimes you are dense. Anyway it's a little like wondering what Scotchmen wear under their kilts."

Since Margaret never had shown any weighty preference for any one of them, her young men had to recognize that it was probable she would marry while they were away at a war which seemed likely to go on who knew how many years (the Japanese had overrun the Philippines, Singapore had fallen ingloriously in two days, the Allied fleet was at the bottom of the Java Sea). It could be that she would marry one of them: absence and the outspokenness that in some relationships is possible only in letters might bring to view chemistry not detectable yet, or lightning might strike on behalf of one of them while he was home on leave.

What they really wanted was for Margaret, while they were away, not to get married and not to get laid and not to get any older and not even to buy any new clothes so that when they got back they could take up with her exactly where they had left off. Almost every one of them was filled with rage at being packed off to this war, at the age of twenty-one or twenty-two when he was entitled to be starting the plummiest years of his life. Unspokenly, they gave Margaret to understand it was up to her whether they were soured on the world for life.

A man going off to battles needs a little magic to support him, they seemed to be saying to her; if you fail to brush your hair exactly one thousand times every night, of if you take a lover and turn on the light to see his face, it may be we shall die, killed by you as surely as if you'd stuck pins in the photographs we are providing you with, framed so that they can be a standing reproach. They knew, though, it was most likely that Margaret would marry some man now unknown to her and to them, some stranger the war would bring to San Diego. In a way this would be preferable.

Out there or over there, it would be better not to know the face of the man with whom Margaret would be in bed, this as-yet shapeless enjoyer of Margaret might appear in any of a number of shapes, all acceptable to the pride of the men overseas: he might be rich and a 4-F, or middle-aged and rich, or middle-aged, and of a higher rank than her contemporaries could hope for; the essential ingredient, from their point of view, in all these combinations or any permutation of them would be that Margaret wouldn't have married the man if her old friends had been around and in competition.

She might of course make one of those unaccountable marriages, so that years after the war they still would be shaking their heads and saying, half-wryly and hoping that what they were implying wasn't true,

[33]

The Duration

that they didn't know what she saw in him (after all, they all had seen one another, in high school gymnasiums and country club lockers, in cabanas beside swimming pools and behind rocks at the beach: everybody knew pretty well how everybody else was fixed.) Or she might be simply swept off her feet—some of the departing young men still hoped that the emotionalism of the times would work in their favor. There was that Irish side of Margaret. The shrewder young men saw that she wasn't a girl who would go to bed with a man because he was going to war, but that she might marry a man for the same reason. Discreetly—there was that mocking side to her too—they displayed the flag, and hoped they might yet see her by the dawns early light.

Harry afforded them none of the balms they had counted on. He didn't even wait to appear until they were overseas. Margaret met him on a blind date. He was large, bland and cheerful; he could not be sneered at for being too handsome or too intelligent; he had a certain air of the Eastern Shore, of a world where foxes still were pursued and Franklin Roosevelt's uncle lived next door, that was impressive in San Diego. Margaret liked this ambience and liked his money, but her old friends suspected she would have married him in any case. Some of them were told so by Margaret, gently but with a touch of feline cruelty, as if she were bandaging up their wounds but couldn't resist giving the bandage a tweak to remind them that they were ailing and she was healthy.

Two weeks after she met Harry some of them had suspected what was going to happen. After four weeks a few became so rattled they proposed to her, more for the sake of finding out where Harry stood than for finding out where they stood, and were given the word, though in so veiled and tentative a fashion that she

[34]

might have been announcing that she was available for nomination to the office of Harry's wife. After six weeks it was official; in three months she was married.

Penelope had looked out the window and seen a man passing by and had yelled, "Help! I'm bored!" and the stranger had heard her and come in, and looked the suitors over, and then shot them dead. But they were still alive, really; they had to give a bachelor dinner for Harry, which was attended by some Navy officers who knew him more or less casually from having worked with him in the offices of the Eleventh Naval District. These men were boisterous in their congratulations, indecent in their speculations about Margaret, and indifferent to or unaware of the magnanimity (represented by this dinner) displayed by Margaret's friends, who were reduced to sulking like the Macedonians at those difficult dinner parties Alexander used to give for the Persians. The defeated suitors attended the wedding; some of them helped to form an arch of swords for the bridal couple. They waited in San Diego, not heroes yet, while Margaret went on her honeymoon.

They wished they were in New Guinea, or Iceland, or Calcutta. When they were, Margaret wrote them proudly that Harry had applied for sea duty. After he went overseas, Margaret's correspondents sweated out the word that she was pregnant. No announcement came, and they began to sweat for other reasons — the Catholics when they thought of her doing un-Catholic things, and as for the Protestants, those who were doing sea duty like Harry had such thoughts it was all they could do (sometimes more than they could do) to keep from buggering the prettier sailors. These were the offenses for which Margaret's old friends now looking for revenge on Harry — a mild revenge; few of them still entertained any substantial hopes; when Harry's being killed, they dimly apprehended, might wall off Margaret irrevocably from her old life. But Edwards observed that the evenings she spent with these men appeared to refresh and brighten Margaret. Maybe she didn't at all mind, a session of hearing Harry minimized; maybe the necessity of being loyal to Harry in all other ways, because she wasn't physically loyal to him, sometimes got on her nerves. But if the failed suitors managed to lull Margaret, for an evening at least, into feeling that Harry didn't alter very much, where did that leave Edwards how much attention would Andromeda have paid to Perseus, if somebody had come and sat on her rock and sweet-talked her about old times and simply ignored the monster, or told her not to bother about it?

In the long run, maybe Edwards had more to gain by keeping Harry a personage in Margaret's eyes than Harry did. Edwards was cast, in the drama going on in Margaret's head as the potential Harry-slayer (even if Harry were really killed, it might seem to Margaret that Edwards had done it), but Harry had to be somebody worth slaying. The war might last six or seven years; and unless Harry was assigned to stateside duty so that a conclusion would be forced there was every danger Margaret would grow tired of Edwards and the situation he had invoked and simply revert to Harry—by default so to speak. It was important to Edwards that Margaret's interior drama be kept at high intensity— she must see herself as choosing between two estimable men, she must believe she would be doing either an important injury by depriving him of herself later, if the verdict went against Harry, Edwards could count on Harry's shriveling up, in Margaret's recollection, into a nonentity; the Marxists who rewrite history should let women do it.

The Duration

Sometimes when Margaret was out with other men, Edwards found himself more indignant with her on Harry's behalf than his own. If somewhere within him there was a nodule of contempt for Margaret because she was unfaithful to Harry, that grain of feeling was quick to aggrandize itself into a statement of principle: she owed it to Harry to maintain his dignity before those fellows. Edwards took a deep pull of his drink. It was time, on every count, for him to be getting out of there. Margaret was still disbursing groceries around the kitchen, a faint impatience in her movements.

She opened the refrigerator, and Edwards' glance fell on the chops. Margaret turned around and saw his hot blue stare.

"Don't be ridiculous," she said. "The chops are for you. Tomorrow night," she laughed.

It tantalized Edwards that he couldn't tell from her remark if she were going out on the town with her date or offering the man dinner here—which was nothing that Edwards could object to, considering the claims of old acquaintance, and how crowded every restaurant and bar was and how poor the fare, and the fact that some of these men who visited Margaret honestly wanted nothing except a familiar face and a common set of memories, a drink in peace and a place to shed the demands or humiliations of rank. The enlisted men among Margaret's friends didn't much relish taking her out, especially remembering that her husband was an officer; there wasn't much saluting these nights in San Francisco, where people pleasure-bent and hurrying through the dim streets jostled one another good-naturedly or angrily, like spectators pouring into a football stadium, but tacitly admitted to a common need to snatch at brief satisfactions which made an ordinary insistence upon status out of the question. Still, occasionally an officer who was alone would stare a salute out of an enlisted man who had a good-looking girl with him.

Edwards, though a civilian, had his own symbols of authority. He shrugged himself into his topcoat, of heavy Orkney tweed. It gave him a solid, authoritative and prosperous look, and a sensation that he possessed exactly those qualities. Margaret responded instantly to the coat, or to the augmentation of confidence the coat gave him. She took hold of its lapels and kissed him.

"You look like a field marshal in that coat," she observed.

He was pleased, but wished she could have found a compliment outside the military idiom. Still, being unable to be a field marshal was a disability he shared with every other American; perhaps Margaret's unconscious tact had been at work, imputing to him glamour beyond the reach of the wearers of commonplace American uniforms. He turned toward the door, his step and manner grave.

"See you tomorrow," Margaret said cheerfully. He thought she sounded as if she were looking forward to the evening ahead—she probably was. Margaret had a great capacity for relishing the moment. Someone who saw her at a party on a houseboat in Richardson's Bay said that no one since Cleopatra could have had so much fun on a barge; the onions in her Gibsons might have been real pearls.

Just as he shut the apartment's front door Margaret's telephone rang. He hesitated, thinking that her date might be cancelled. Margaret's heels clacked across the floor, their briskness seeming to suggest she had put Edwards out of her mind. He heard her answer the phone. Her voice was warm and leonine, except in this greeting. He supposed girls, when they began having calls from boys, cultivated a style of answering the phone; Margaret had settled on an impatient manner, and deepening and roughening her voice in a way which obviously destined her to spend a lot of time in the future explaining that she wasn't her husband, whoever he then might be. Edwards listened to her, talking cheerfully, but couldn't make out many words. The dignity of his coat asserted itself, and he headed for the stairs. Unfortunately no one saw him leaving. It was a wasted opportunity for impressing on spectators the respectability of his relations with Margaret, It was barely past seven, and here he was on his way out; and nobody at all saw him.

[FOUR]

He went out into the night. If Margaret, as the apartment door closed, had experienced a relief from the pressure he exerted upon her, it was Edwards' turn to be lightened when the building's door clicked shut behind him. He could do what he liked: he stood on the sidewalk fingering his ticket to Ludlow Fair, the complimentary admission to lovely muck handed to a man by a woman who puts him out of the house. The wartime city was a muddied pond, its depths dimly lit; Edwards wondered what he wanted to fish for tonight. He let his feet carry him down one hill and up another, pacing off the San Francisco blocks whose shortness and tiptiltedness kept spring in the walkers' steps; these were pavements you could not pound. He emerged in the elegant little square on which the Fairmont and Mark Hopkins hotels face. Young officers, furred girls on their arms, hurried toward the hotels' portals. Margaret might shortly be among them, but Edwards was benign toward them. He was older than most of them and was glad to feel himself so and to be at home in a city that lay as open to him as wicked London to a Gerald Kersh character.

He could go to a Chinese nightclub, whose Chinese owner was a friend of his and would insist on buying him drinks and be offended if he left without enjoying a Chinese girl or girls. (In an ultimate, adult parody of a childhood pleasure, they swung toward you in a giant swing, enclosed you and swung away again; they put a ball of silk into your body and unraveled it at the moment of orgasm.)

He could drink in Izzy Gomez' bar, a sawdust-strewn little room upstairs in a rundown rooming house; behind the bar, Izzy, a Portuguese mulatto, devoted father of thirteen children, never seen without a sweat-stained brown hat that blended into his own color; on your right at the bar might be Lionel, Lord Tennyson, or Lawrence Tibbett; on your left a bum attracted by the good bourbon that Izzy still served for twenty cents.

He could drink in the bar owned by Rene Sarraut, a sculptor who one night had suggested to Margaret that he sculpt her torso, nude; when Margaret laughed and shook her head, Rene turned to Edwards: "You wouldn't care to let me do *your* torso, sometime?"

There was a cappuccino bar in North Beach where he'd be likely to run into a relation of William Saroyan's, who lately had cut off a toe: whether by accident or as a venture into the Van Gogh sphere — testing the bath with a toe so to speak — Edwards didn't know.

If he telephoned right now, he could spend the evening with a girl who appeared to resent her husband's having left her (by the Army's choice, not his) only six weeks after they had been married and she had lost her virginity. She encouraged sexual variety; she

[41]

made love as if posing for a postcard, one of a set which after the war she would hand to her husband: <u>there</u>! He could have at her with a barbarousness and relish it was becoming somewhat difficult for him to achieve with Margaret, to whom he was either too nearly married or not married enough. Or, he knew where there was a poker game.

He could dine at Tadich's Cold Day Grill, where the rex sole never had heard of wartime austerity and the wrinkled, shriveled Yugoslav bartender shook with age but never spilled a drop, and then stroll downtown and take what the evening brought him. In this city overflowing with manless women there was no need for a man of any enterprise to resort to commercial talent, but Edwards sometimes was tempted, out of curiosity and respect for her ingenuity, to patronize the good-looking woman of about thirty who'd found a way to conduct her trade openly on the humanity-jammed sidewalks of Market, the city's busiest street. Dressed in the stylish gray-green uniform of the American Women's Voluntary Services (a title which must have provided her with some amusement), perfectly looking the part of a young matron doing her bit for the war effort, she stood among the crowds passing out pamphlets on first aid or air raid precautions or how to help win the war by growing your own vegetable garden; she watched the crowd carefully and when she saw a man she judged to be prosperous and in a mood to buy she handed him a pamphlet and as she did so leaned quickly toward his ear and murmured: "Would you like to sleep with me?" Edwards admired her enormously. (He hoped and trusted that she really was commercial and wasn't just doing it for the fun of it.) It would be worth paying her just to get to know her.

The Duration

Or he might go to Malloy's, downstairs in the *Observer* Building, a bar totally without attractions except that it sold liquor—even its credit policy, though as a newspaperman's bar it had to give credit, was not generous. The owner, who worked behind the bar, was building a $300,000 home in Hillsborough, where he would live cheek by jowl with utility company presidents.

In this bar Edwards could drink with his peers: a long evening of comment, appraisal, criticism, news, shop talk, gossip, elegies for the departed, with footnotes whittling them down to size, and anecdotes which the speaker, reliving in his memories, told with an air of amusement and incredulity at his past successes in outwitting women, employers and colleagues, all of whom, it was clear to the listeners, now had his number. Edwards enjoyed sometimes spending an evening in this way. He liked newspapermen but even when himself a cub hadn't found them glamorous. He thought they were endearing. In spite of their intelligence and their knowledge of life as seen from the inside or underside, they remained oddly naive.

Hearing them talk was like listening to the affairs of the Ottoman Empire discussed by the inmates of the sultan's harem; they knew so much other people didn't know, their knowledge entitled them to be comical and mirthful and coarse about the great, and yet their sense of reality was faulty: they lacked a feeling for how things really are done in the world. Edwards thought it was because, in harem or city room, the personnel never handled or were possessed of much money, but still found themselves treated as being of some consequence: it threw their understanding of cause and effect out of kilter. Sometimes being persons to be wooed, they failed to see that mostly they were only persons to be screwed; the most fun they had in life was in these evenings of exchanging confidences with one another.

Edwards was able to enjoy these evenings more than many of his coworkers because of his small cushion of an income and because he wasn't married. His pleasure wasn't marred by the realization that when the next round came around he would either have to borrow from a fellow drinker or ask credit from the house, or by guilt and unease because he was drinking up the household money. (On the other hand, these drinking nights didn't have quite the edge and tension for him that his friends experienced. They knew the happiness of the drinker, threatened with being cut off in mid-course, who suddenly finds himself restored and rearmed with a borrowed five-dollar bill. They were on leave from a front on which they already could hear tomorrow's guns muttering, while he sat among them like a staff officer. They couldn't afford to be bored, because they couldn't afford the evening at all.)

Edwards concealed the fact that he had an outside source of income, but it didn't take the other drinkers long to notice that he never appeared to be broke. He was reasonably generous about buying drinks for colleagues who found themselves short, but he was careful about lending money, partly by instinct and training, and partly from a suspicion that trying to staunch the financial hemophilia of his friends could become as unhappy a commitment as being family physician to Philoctetes. He evolved an unstated policy of not letting anyone get into him for more than ten dollars. To head off requests for loans or imputations of ungenerosity, he never entered Malloy's with more than five dollars visible in his wallet; the rest was tucked away in a back pocket of his trousers, from which another bill could be withdrawn in the privacy of the men's room if the evening seemed to warrant it.

Edwards had been working for the *Observer* eighteen months before Jack Cunningham, the night editor, would borrow money from him. On quiet nights, after eleven, Cunningham sometimes would come downstairs to the bar and spend half an hour or more. Occasionally he was out of funds, but though he might be sitting and talking with Edwards, to whom he seemed to enjoy doling out small measures of disparagement and mockery, if he needed money he would ask the bartender to put his drinks on the cuff or look around the house for a rewrite man or one of the older photographers to put the bite on. One night he asked Edwards to lend him three dollars, refusing with distaste the five-spot Edwards hastily extracted from a back pocket and offered him.

"Three dollars is what I need," he said, coldly and dismissingly.

Cunningham paid the money back on payday, and it was six months before he asked Edwards for a loan again, but Edwards realized that he had passed some milepost of acceptance.

Edwards was standing now looking, from the edge of the plateau on Nob Hill's top, down Mason Street. Up its sidewalks, tilted like a fire ladder, two or three festive couples huffed and puffed toward the hilltop hotels and their joys; if as children they had sometimes climbed the wrong way up playground slides they would have had the right sort of training for this street. Edwards was just outside the gates which led into the small forecourt of the Mark Hopkins, where taxis and other cars paused to unload passengers and were waved on by a doorman in an imperial frenzy, whistling like a tugboat. The cars emerging from the court turned into California Street

and plunged downhill; this descent had a certain quality of irrevocability about it, like going down a playground slide. The forecourt and the hotel's front
entrance were on a level with Huntington Square, which
is the top of Nob Hill, but the hotel's foundations were
far down the hillside; towering over its neighbors, it
nevertheless looked as if its squarely Italianate rival
across the street, the Fairmont, had given it a good push
off the top of the hill, but hadn't been able to dislodge it
from the slope to which it clung.

Even though those couples toiling up the hill didn't
know he'd been evicted from Margaret's apartment—
and they were so ostentatiously gay it seemed as if they
must know, and were bent on rubbing in the contrast
between him and themselves—Edwards didn't want, in
any case, to appear to them like a man who had nothing
to do and nobody to do it with (ridiculous, he told himself, hastily telling over again the rich possibilities he
just had been considering) so he stood rocking on his
heels as if he were waiting for someone; this increased
his sensation of waiting for inclination to give him a
push.

As he teetered Edwards realized that his relief at
his temporary freedom from Margaret had embold-
ened his resentments to rise in a jacquerie, howling for
true abolition of women. He wanted the soothing sensation of drinking among men, where women, if they
were mentioned, could be handled boldly and creative-
ly. On the other hand, he didn't like to go to Malloy's
at this hour—it was now seven-forty—for much the
same reason that he hadn't wanted to look like a loner
to the couples who were now crossing the forecourt of
the Mark, their evening's pleasure perhaps increased
.005 percent by the fact that there had been a friendless
spectator to watch them as they skipped into the play-

ground. A bachelor of twenty-seven however voluntary his condition, can be surprisingly sensitive about
his state, especially in a time of pairing-off such as the
outbreak of a war; in Edwards' case these (occasional)
feelings were aggravated by his civilian condition.
There was a great difference between sitting and drinking in Malloy's for two and a half hours after getting
off work, and in reappearing there two and a half hours
after leaving the city room, confessedly a man with no
place else to go.

Besides, men have a cruelly keen instinct for detect-
ing sexual wounds, just inflicted by a woman; going
among other men in such a condition can be like bleed-
ing among sharks. Edwards, a fellow who needed a
friend, decided he would call Malloy's and see if Lucius
Ramirez was there, which was fairly probable since it
was Wednesday; on Mondays and Tuesdays Lucius was
apt to be suffering from the languors and scars of the
weekend, those strenuousities might or might not have
included a fight with his wife, and he would head for
home early; he lived in Los Altos, a fairly long com-
mute, which he could make by car only because he had
a photographer's "C" gas ration card. Fridays too he
was off for home without much pause, ready for the
pleasures and strifes of another weekend. But on
Wednesdays and Thursdays he was likely in his home-
ward passage to get lodged in Malloy's, sometimes in
the mood of the happy vagabond's singing to hell with
Burgundy, sometimes in the mood of Father Hopkins'
nun seeking shelter from storms, and sometimes in the
mood of the accident-prone. ("Never telephone them to
say you'll be late," he once advised Edwards. "Why get
bit twice?")

Edwards walked into the Mark's lobby and went
into a telephone booth. As soon as he had fished a nick-

el out of his pocket he was seized by a powerful and humiliating urge—possibly owing something to the nature of a telephone booth, a place redolent of loneliness and lust, traditionally the scene of obscene actions—to call Margaret and see if she and her date were spending the evening at home. His self-regard, which prevented him from calling, was aided by the consideration that she'd certainly see through whatever excuse he might invent for calling—calling and hanging up when she answered would rate him with a peeping tom, in his own eyes and hers, while the circumstance that she couldn't be absolutely sure it wasn't a wrong number simply would make her angrier with him. He also was helped, in resisting his impulse to call, by having only one nickel: spending it and then having to go over to the newsstand to get change to call Lucius would somehow, by its sheer unnecessariness, make the silliness of that call look sillier. He dialed Malloy's and asked for Lucius.

Lucius came to the phone bravely and quickly. The Spanish pride and fatalism of his father's forebears, or the Swedish stolidity and suicidal- impulses of his mother's side would never allow him to ask if it was a woman calling.

"Ramirez," he said into the horn, undaunted as Roland.

"You going to be there for about fifteen minutes?" Edwards asked.

"What's your plot?" Lucius wanted to know. His voice, after a few drinks, became rich and plummy; it also contained an exhilaration, momentarily threatening to become airborne, which sometimes appeared in his pictures, such as a famous one he took one summer Sunday at Fleishhacker Zoo, of a solemnly bounding kangaroo, an animal which could have appealed to him because of the way it had managed to combine family responsibility with a life of motion. His tone, at present, also was slightly cautious; he probably had been nearly ready to start home, and feared being deflected by Edwards.

"Nothing much," Edwards said, trying to keep his tone light. He didn't want to sound lonely and in need of succor, because he didn't feel that way; or more exactly, he did feel that way, but he would be constrained to deny that this feeling of rejection was the major element in his mood (which remained on the whole, one of readiness to kick up his heels in pastures he hadn't visited lately); just as Lucius, who was about fifteen years older than Edwards and was a liberal who soon would be a relic of the spirit of the mid-1930s would be constrained to deny that the fact that the republican government of Spain included Communists made it a Communist government. Since Lucius must realize that Margaret for some reason wasn't at home to Edwards this evening, Edwards' voice had acquired strain just from the effort of trying not to sound forlorn.

"If you're not set on going home, I thought we might eat at Tadich's," he added.

The line's other end was silent while Lucius thought.

Edwards pictured him: olive-skinned and chunky, in a soberly and Castilianly black suit; considering the round head and the short nose and the heavy black-rimmed glasses, you could only say owlish; the face was slightly swollen with good living, and in the mornings sometimes was an owl's who was having trouble with the indigestible parts of last night's mice. While he stood and thought at the end of the bar where the phone was he would be taking small delicate puffs at his cigarette holder or crooking it at an elegant angle in his free hand. Edwards couldn't decide if the provenance of this holder was Spanish or Rooseveltian. The dainty and slightly tentative manner in which Lucius fitted cigarettes into the holder said Castile, but the jaunty grip his teeth took on it was Hyde Park.

Lucius said: "I'll be here, but let's make it soon." Edwards promised to be present in twenty minutes. Lucius seldom arrived at a rendezvous on time — there was always a martini waiting somewhere to pluck at his sleeve — and tended to ascribe this failing to others. He was, beneath the blandness and self-possession, secretly a keen student and critic of his owl character; his eminence in this field made him feel himself an authority on the nature of other people: he was in fact a shrewd and kindly man. Probably he really wanted to go home; Edwards never truly blamed himself for being a bachelor, but sometimes he had to give himself low marks (as he did now, the minute he hung up the phone) for exhibiting a bachelor's selfishness.

Lucius worried a good deal about his health. His mother, a Nebraska schoolteacher and Populist reformer, had implanted in him a thoroughgoing materialism. (This may have been why he became a photographer; it comforted him and confirmed him in his view of the world, when he developed his negatives, never to discover anything there for which he couldn't account.) Nevertheless, Lucius was Spanish too, and had a sense of sin, and sometimes suffered over his drinking. His repentance took the form of hypochondria. He went, as if to the confessional, to his doctor, who prescribed — not penances, but a visit to the drugstore, where they sold indulgences. The glove compartments of most cameramen's cars contained spare flashbulbs. Lucius' glove compartment was full of pill bottles. The only form of medical reassurance

from which he shied away was X-rays; he was willing
to appear before the doctors as an anxious child, and
be pampered and comforted with any cosset they
could devise, but he was damned if they were going to
work white magic (and charge him for it) in his own
medium. Besides, if he were shown a photograph of
some ailment within him it would surely kill him. His
faith in physicians had its limits, but he trusted cameras. There would be no appeal from a photograph's
verdict.

Home, to Lucius, was a good deal more than a
place he went when he wasn't feeling well. He had a
Spaniard's sense of the value of home, and a Swede's
sense of the value of a home port. He had his own balance and adjustments which kept him from flying
apart, but they were oiled and kept in good repair by
his blonde and humorous wife, who from the first
days of their marriage had been the occasion of deep
rejoicing within him. She pleased his Spanish self's
taste for blonde women and his Swedish self's taste for
blonde women. If the Spanish component had har-
bored any guilty belief that it was indulging its low
inclinations by marrying a blonde, these feelings had
been smoothed away by the remarkable circumstance
that though she was a Nebraskan of antecedents more
Lutheran than Luther, she had decided early that she
didn't like her name, which was Anna, and romanti-
cally had elided it into Ana. It wasn't that she was
especially interested in Spain; she simply wanted to
change her name, and do it in the most economical
way and with the least fuss possible. Lucius believed
that chance was as blind as Justice, so he could only
conclude that Ana's inclination toward the Spanish
was much deeper than she consciously realized. It was
a fundamentally reassuring thought.

The Duration

There was a reason for Lucius to be deeply impressed by Ana's feat in changing her name. His own name had been subject to alteration, but by others, when he was an infant; he had been saved from a lot of grief. His mother, whose education had been classical, wanted to name him for Lucillus, whom she admired as a farmer and as a reformer. His father argued that no one could live with a name like that, especially not in Nebraska. They compromised by calling the baby Lucius (for Lucius Licinius Lucullus), a name which was acceptable to his father's Southwestern antecedents.

His father was a New Mexican of good family; a younger son, who had chosen to live the life of a wandering cowhand until he wandered up to Nebraska, where he met and married a pretty schoolteacher and settled down on a small cattle ranch, bought with an inheritance which had been sitting unused for years in a bank in Santa Fe.

Lucius had grown up in the early years of the motion picture. The fantasy of movies naturally was triple in its effect in that dull little Nebraska town; but it sometimes made Lucius uncomfortable that the Westerns nearly always resolved themselves in a manner that closely resembled his parent's story — the cowboy married the schoolteacher. This disconcerting perception, which he kept to himself and hoped had not occurred to his friends, intensified in him the feeling natural to all adolescents that their parents are ridiculously out of date; it was an early taste in his mouth which contributed to his essentially wry view of life — it set the teeth on edge to be named Lucius and to have narrowly escaped being named Lucullus, to have parents who were straight out of a William S. Hart plot.

If Lucius took anything seriously, aside from photographs, it was money. His respect for it sprang naturally from his mother's materialism and populism. The essence of reform, for her, was to spread more money around among more people. Lucius felt the same way, which was why he had been, for some time, a Newspaper Guild organizer. Lucius' regard for money was one reason why he was waiting for Edwards tonight. Faintly but unmistakably, he was impressed by Edwards. He knew perfectly well that Edwards had no *money*, as distinct from money; he knew Edwards' parents were something short of being rich; he had only a vague idea of Edwards' connection, through his mother, with the feudal Spanish Californians. Nevertheless he felt that Edwards had an entree. (That was the word Lucius would have used; his mother had given him a sound, elegant, old-fashioned education.)

Though this was true, it also was true that it was kind of him to wait for Edwards tonight, when almost certainly he would rather have gone home.

Yielding to the weakness which Lucius erroneously had ascribed to him—to be blamed, unjustly, for a fault is always license and encouragement to commit it— Edwards decided to have a drink before he left the Mark. He went into the bar off the lobby; it was a cold and heavily gilded room which repelled tourists. The only drinkers were a Scots officer in kilts, standing at the bar and talking to the bartender, and two young Navy officers at a table, who seemed as hysterically amused at the Scotsman's bare knees as if his skirts implied some derogation of their own manhood. Edwards put his drink down quickly and said good-night to the bartender, whose name was Halter and who had never regretted leaving Montana, as he had told Edwards many times and had just told the Scotsman.

The Duration

It was a briskly pleasant walk down the hill, and down Geary Street and across Market to Malloy's, but Edwards should have taken a cab. When he got to Malloy's Lucius was three-quarters stiff, Lucius, when in this condition, regarded himself with detachment and gentle alarm, rather as if he were a large mother bird trying to shoo himself out of harm's way

"Fried," he clucked or mildly hooted. "I'm fried." While they considered this, they had two more drinks. Deciding it was prudent to leave Lucius' car where it was parked, they went out into the street to look for a cab, not easy to find at nine o'clock in a war-jammed city where most private cars were immobilized by gas rationing. (The cab drivers' attitude approximated that of the serfs after the Black Death had created a labor shortage; they roared through the streets, ignoring hails, carrying Boccaccio and his friends safely out of a city full of the plague-stricken.)

The only cab that would stop for them already had two couples in it who were going to a party in the Marina, so Edwards and Lucius rode with them to their destination and then backtracked to Tadich's, where they arrived just in time to be told, with stern Slavic scorn for all drinkers whose heads hadn't been hardened by early exposure to vodka or slivovitz, that it was closing.

A chain of such happenings seems like a command to keep on drinking. Edwards and Lucius began to move in the general direction of a restaurant in North Beach, stopping at bars on the way. They wound up, after midnight when the bars closed, eating hamburgers and drinking coffee at a counter. Lucius stared straight ahead as if he had been told he had cancer which furthermore would spread to all his negatives and destroy them too.

The Duration

He put down his coffee cup and, still staring at the huge painted menu on the wall behind the counter, said to Edwards: "I don't think I can make it home."

"Better not try," Edwards answered, with the easy wisdom of the bachelor.

They made their way, laborious and cautious as climbers on Everest, up steep Russian Hill to Edwards' apartment. A mist had appeared while they were eating; it mingled with the sweat on their faces and blurred the street lights, reinforcing their alcoholic sense that reality had receded from them slightly. In the apartment Lucius decided that his rule no longer applied and called his home in Los Altos. Edwards went into the bathroom, ran water noisily and flushed the toilet; deciding all this tact was too ostentatious — tact, like any other characteristic, can become larger than life under the influence of alcohol — he went back into the living room, but the call was over.

Lucius was having a drink. The phone had been answered by his eleven-year-old daughter (Ana slept like a farm hand). "That girl gets more like her mother every day," he remarked.

Edwards went to a closet and found sheets and a blanket. He handed them to Lucius, who neatly and skillfully made up the Hollywood bed in the living room. Lucius stripped to his shorts — previous evenings of this sort had shown that he was too plump to get into a pair of Edwards' pajamas — and climbed into the bed, where he lay on his back, smoking. Edwards put out the light and said goodnight. The cigarette, glowing at the end of the holder in the dark above Lucius' head, moved in a red arc as Lucius took the holder out of his mouth to answer. "Oh Christ," he said.

Edwards dreamed he was arguing with Margaret. She insisted there was no such name as Harry. Nothing

The Duration

Edwards said convinced her. He belabored her with learning; Harry was an old name, he told her, one of the oldest in the language; it was originally a forest god's, the old Harry. Margaret looked as if she thought he were inventing this. Look at Shakespeare, he argued: the plays are full of people talking about Harry the Fifth or Harry the Eighth. "I thought it was Hal," Margaret said.

[FIVE]

Fall in San Francisco was Edwards' favorite season. The weather there is best in September: blue skies and mild, warm days after the coastal fogs of July and August in which the tourists have shivered, sour and unreconciled to their condition as wet cats. At this time of year an old rhythm took hold of Edwards. As a child he had spent his summers on a small ranch in San Mateo County which his grandmother owned. On the last day before the family went back to the city he would walk around the ranch for a formal leave-taking of his pony, the horses, the dogs, the cows, the cats, the creek that would be dry then but would still have a little winter water in it when he came back next June.

Animals seemed to live a long time at his grandmother's, possibly because she cared little about them. She was a thoroughly urban woman who had bought the ranch as a whim, or to assert herself against her children or in favor of her grandchildren. She had no pets and made few demands on the animals. Edwards could be calm in the certainty of next June and of all being unchanged. Next day he would be ready to welcome the excitement of a new season. He was aware of the pageant of the autumn city flaming with the energy released by seasonal ritual: what had ripened in the summer was ready to spend itself in these streets filled with limousines, doormen, women in furs; Market Street at the five o'clock rush hour was jammed solid with streetcars, four files of them; windows in Telegraph Hill apartment houses reflected yellow light from the autumn sun as it sank into an unspanned Golden Gate; a few cars moved through the quiet evening streets of Pacific Heights while his mother's second maid pulled the curtains against the dark; the calendars read 1923 or 1925 or 1927.

It wasn't like that for San Franciscans in 1943. They were, if they had known it, in the trough of the war. Whatever charm of novelty the conflict may have had was gone. Men who had never noticed that their fathers or their wives were growing old became acutely conscious of mortality as all the automobiles that one saw became older and needed paint worse and throbbed with the threat of possibly fatal defeats. No new houses were built. More and more women went barelegged as silk or nylon stockings became more precious. Wives developed new marriages, conducted entirely on paper; each adjusted her personality as a letter writer to the personality of her husband as a letter writer sometimes they wondered wildly what had become of the men they thought they remembered, who had so little in common with these correspondents who with Stuart stubbornness maintained across the water their pretensions to rights that certainly had been vacated — that might be empty?

The Duration

The wives speculated whether their marriages were real, and if they would recognize and cheer the Pretender when he came ashore, his flagstaff raised. The news in newspapers hadn't even the redeeming qualities of disaster, which tones up the system and can be blamed on somebody; it was technically good, like vitamins, but tasteless. Russian troops retook from the Germans three villages a day and one important railroad center a week. Allied troops moved or didn't move up Italy, bloody river crossing by bloody river crossing. The Japanese, stubborn as badgers in their dens, were flushed out of island after island which few people knew they had seized or been seized of; few could tingle at the news of the fall of Palau or Ulithi. (Edwards' glance, as he was leaving the city room late one night, was caught by some writing in French on a scrap of paper lying on the rim of the copy desk. It was a head somebody'd written for his own amusement. "MacArthur le Magnifique a Tombé sur une Autre Ile," it said.) How long would it take to get to Berlin and Tokyo, when even Rome was so hard of attainment? More and more people knew somebody who had been killed.

In the harbor a throbbing of purpose could be felt, signs of growing military strength were visible, but most of the city's inhabitants were too immersed in their own concerns to notice. At the Fort Mason docks, where the troops embarked, there were often as many as three transports tied up at once; the old single-funnelled transports built in the '20s or earlier, looking diminished in their wartime gray covering the gleaming white hulls and multi-colored funnels of before the war, and the converted passenger liners now were being joined by the big new two-stacked transports laid down especially for the Army Transport Service.

Liberty ships, the workhorse cargo- and troop-carriers, were being succeeded on the shipyards' ways by the larger Victory ships. "Jeeps," the little 10,000-ton escort aircraft carriers which basically were nothing but a flight deck imposed on the hull of a cargo vessel, were being turned out by the yards in increasing numbers. (In a hundred bars the shipyard workers told the story of the escort carrier, being built for the Royal Navy, whose British skipper when he arrived to inspect his new command insisted that the yard tear out the shower in his quarters and install a proper bathtub.) The great gray-painted shapes of the Queen Mary and Queen Elizabeth, ferrying troops to Australia, became known in the port.

Among those unmoved and unimpressed by this massing thunderhead of power was Margaret. She had become antagonistic to the war; a personal antagonism; she wasn't simply against the abstraction, war, she had developed a thoroughly womanly dislike for this particular war. She had a good womanly reason: it had disillusioned her. She couldn't understand, now, how she ever could have admired it or been erotically stirred by it; she had divorced it, on the witness stand she had detailed the mental cruelty inflicted on once bright, trusting, virginal Margaret, who in 1940 had been starry-eyed over the heroism of the Royal Air Force, who next year bought albums of recorded Red Army songs and after Pearl Harbor wrote a poem to Colin Kelly. Once she had seen war as a possible opportunity for male gloriousness; now she knew it represented male obtuseness, male futility, and the male obsessions with custom and ritual, with blood, sweat and sentimentality, and with statistics (all bores to women, even on the playing fields of Eton, but a horror when they erupted into Waterloo). She also suspected a profound male relief at escaping from the sexual demands of women.

Margaret mostly refused, these days, to read newspapers. She felt as if the whole of every newspaper had turned into a giant sports section, which a woman could only stare at blankly and then pass across the table to a man, for whom it would have some meaning. The enthusiasms, the struggles, the triumphs reported in print seemed to her something apart from life; something to be waited out, as a woman might wait out a baseball broadcast on a Saturday afternoon.

She carefully read, though, the San Francisco news in the *Observer*, because these stories might have been written by Edwards or been part of his day in some way. As long as she was Edwards' girl there was no pleasure she would deny him; obscurely she felt that she owed him the best of all possible times, since she might have to take all this good fortune away from and bestow it back on Harry. Meanwhile he would be Edwards' little cavewoman, crouching meekly by the fire, mixing martinis for him and listening to him add five feet to the tusks of the mammoth which almost had fallen into his snare. Edwards wouldn't have enjoyed so much explaining to her the fine points of stories he had written if she hadn't already read them and missed the fine points. She recognized it as necessary that occasionally she should detect a fine point by herself without being coached; it showed she was taking an interest and was learning. The most delicate enjoyment they ever exchanged was a flicker of complicity, signaling awareness that she was more knowledgeable and critical concerning Edwards' work — she had been editor of her college newspaper — than it suited either of them to concede.

Though she wouldn't read about the war, Margaret listened at least twice a day to war news on the radio.

[61]

The Duration

This was both a practical precaution, like checking the weather, and an obligation. She needed to estimate the chances of Harry's coming home soon on leave, balancing the official news from the Pacific against hints dropped in his letters and information given her by his friends on their way to or from the war. She liked the radio reports because they were brief but presumably touched on everything essential; she wasn't interested in following the course of the war, but if anything should happen to Harry—never just a wound—she wouldn't want to think afterward that at the moment when it happened she hadn't even known about the sea battle or assault on some atoll in which Harry had suffered hurt or worse. She could contemplate, because she had to, the picture of Harry expiring while firmly believing in her fidelity; but she was damned if she was going to have him perish in the delusion: that she was trembling for the safety of his life and limb when really she was only worrying about what to give Edwards for dinner. Not asking Edwards for help, she tried to puzzle out from the war news what hazards Harry might be enduring, and when she believed that he was in danger she tried to remind herself of it at least once an hour. Neither death nor Harry was going to catch her unaware.

The possibility of Harry's early death was like the certainty of her own ultimate death not to be examined too closely; but not for the same reasons. Harry's death wouldn't mean, as her own death would mean, the blotting out of a world; she knew that she could go on without Harry. But it was true, of Harry's death as of her own, that it couldn't be studied too long because to examine it roused too many unanswerable questions. How could she say what Harry's death would mean to her when she didn't know what Harry meant to her? If

Harry should be called upon to provide the answer to both questions, she might not be able to avoid feeling — grief releases many irrationalities not all of which are so irrational — that he had been a victim of her uncertainty, sacrificed to her need to know. It had been Harry's decision to apply for sea duty — a male decision; but involving some wifely acquiescence. The lady who threw her handkerchief into the lion-filled arena wasn't only testing her lover's mettle; she also wanted to find out what she would feel at the prospect the lions might eat him.

Sometimes Margaret would go down into some basement of her being among the withered brooms and old paint cans and broken toilets of realism, and say to herself: Harry's death would make everything so easy. But — before she even had a chance to shudder away from the ugliness of this reflection, which was a shock like her face suddenly seen in a dusty and cracked old mirror — a rat in the corner squeaked that Harry's death might make everything hopelessly difficult; dead Harry might be always with her and Edwards, as impossible to ignore as the stare of a thin, ragged child through a restaurant window.

One night in bed she was unable not to say to Edwards: "Here we are, and right at this minute Harry may be being killed or getting wounded, fighting for his country." If she had not intended to pile on the "fighting for his country" bit, but once she was launched on this sentence she seemed compelled to follow it out to its brutal and banal conclusion. Edwards lay naked beside her and said nothing.

They had been having good fun; she was glad to see that Edwards, though plainly wounded, was not wounded enough to get up and put his clothes on. Of course he couldn't understand that her taunt wasn't aimed at him. There were times when she was quite willing to hurt Edwards, for the trouble he was causing her, but she never would strike at him in that particular way.

She never doubted that he would be playing soldier boy if he could; she knew the damage suffered by his pride because he couldn't be in the war; she was aware of this wound's extent and tenderness in exactly the way a nurse might be aware of, and be careful of, the injury beneath the bandages worn by a patient who had got his hurt in some disreputable way. As a woman Margaret thought Edwards was foolish to mind being a civilian, but she regarded herself as being as thoroughly professional a woman as a nurse is professional as a nurse, and she would never attack Edwards in a way calculated to damage his health. She was incapable of hitting below the belt, in any sense; she thought *Lysistrata* was a thoroughly immoral play, but not for the reasons that her mother, for instance, would have thought so. Her bitter words to Edwards in bed had been aimed entirely at herself; and furthermore their bitterness was spurious and stagy: she knew she was trying to flog herself into feeling what she believed she ought to feel. It didn't work, and she sank happily back into sensuality.

When Edwards made love to her a few minutes later she crossed her legs over his back in a way he liked. Edwards, of course, thought she was just being nice to him to make up for what she had said. Their physical love had been tautened tightened, brought to a new high pitch by the circumstance that Harry very nearly had come home on leave. Or at least they and he had thought be was coming home—the Navy, that grim abstraction which loomed in their sex lives like a father figure telling Harry he was too young to go to bed with girls, telling Edwards he was unfit and so no fit escort for a nice girl like Margaret — may always have known it had no intention of letting go of Harry.

Harry's ship came home to Mare Island for refitting, as his letters had hinted it might; but Harry stayed behind, assigned to another ship by superiors who valued his worth and had small pity on his balls. The small pity consisted of thirty days' leave in Auckland.

Margaret should have been angry with the Navy, but instead she was furious with Harry. When she read the letter in which he said it was pretty well certain that he was coming home her first sensation had been panic: the moment of choice, of confrontation, possibly of exposure and scorn, was upon her. She read on, and came to a rather coarse sentence — this was unlike Harry, who usually was endearingly proper in his letters; he couldn't forget that an officer whom he saw daily would read them to guard against security breaches — in which her husband described what he intended to do on first arriving home.

She thanked god that Edwards wasn't there when she read this letter; the sensation that swept her on reading this blunt sentence was as private as what the words described. She shivered pleasurably at the thought that within a month she might find herself in bed with a man who would be half a stranger to her, and starved for sex; it would be a kind of rape, and the more enjoyable because it would be a rape she was legally and morally bound not to resist, a *droit de siegneur*. She had not realized that there was one pleasure Edwards could not afford her: he was not her lord and master who could tell her to lie on her back. Her shiver deepened as she realized that it might happen that in the space of twenty-four hours she would go to bed with two men, Edwards now would have to stop coming to her apartment, of course she couldn't have Harry arriving home and finding them in bed; but she would break her rule and go to Edwards' place (leaving early enough to get home at a respectable hour, in case Harry should turn up): it would be too mean to deny Edwards what possibly he would never have again. She meant that he should enjoy her up to the last possible moment.

She already was feeling a little guilty about Edwards: no matter how it all turned out, he would suffer a lot while she was sleeping with Harry. Her sense of guilt was increased by the fact that she was enjoying, a little, the idea of Edwards suffering; the trace of resentment she always had felt against him, because he had persuaded or dominated her into committing adultery, was about to exact its pound of Edwards' flesh. It might be that these were the only terms on which she could make the ultimate award of herself to Edwards; that she owed it to her self-respect, or some more savage instinct, to make him wait on her pleasure (and Harry's pleasure; certainly something was owed to Harry; a few days in the hay at least).

Edwards would have to pay a price for her - a bridal price. If she presented herself to Edwards, it would be to an Edwards made fully cognizant of what he might have lost. It wasn't that she would choose to humiliate or injure or humble Edwards; but since it was inevitable that these things should happen to him, she couldn't help seeing some advantages to be gained from these inflictions upon him.

Margaret knew that Edwards was alive to all the nuances involved in Harry's sleeping with her; both Harry considered as husband and Harry considered as soldier home from the wars. Harry, when he came home might be living in a world about to fall in around him; but he'd have his hour, a young man's triumph somewhere on the scale whose high note breaking into frenzy is Alexander at Persepolis: the calm confidence that he was possessing his own, in an act to be repeated many times in years ahead, might lend ease and assurance to Harry's stroke, vigor to his organ. Who could say that Margaret would be unimpressed, unconvinced, by ease, assurance, vigor? Edwards couldn't, Margaret couldn't. Edwards, too, would draw distress from the fact that Harry had earned the right to this manful pleasure by the manful act of defending his country, a title to the enjoyment of Margaret which Edwards didn't possess.

Another man might have asked her not to sleep with Harry, to present him with a fait accompli, tell him it was all over, but Margaret knew that Edwards wouldn't; and that he wouldn't, oddly enough, because of his sense of decency and what was right. Edwards, neither husband nor soldier, couldn't ask her not to go to bed with Harry, much as he might hope that she wouldn't. Margaret respected his respect for Harry's privileges as a husband, and had no admiration at all for his respect for Harry's privileges as a returned warrior. She meant to sleep with Harry because he was a husband who had been away for a long time, not because he was a man in uniform who had been away for a long time. On a more fundamental level, she felt that Edwards was profoundly silly not to try to keep her out of the hay with Harry. It was unthinkable that she'd agree to hold off Harry from his due; but how could Edwards be sure that she wouldn't agree, how could *she* be sure that she wouldn't agree, if Edwards didn't try to command, persuade, cajole her into saying no to Harry?

It might seem curious that it was her lover who appeared as champion of the proprieties—Harry, bent on laying her, seemed by contrast an unscrupulous figure—

but that was an accident of the times, which miscast everybody as badly as the Army did, which made cooks out of graduate physicists. There was a reason she contemplated half-amusedly, with the smile of a woman who'd like to confide in another woman, why she sometimes wished that Edwards simply would forbid her to have anything to do with Harry. She was afraid of betraying involuntarily to Harry that she'd been to bed with another man.

She was more learned now than when Harry had left. It wasn't that Harry was so orthodox in bed—he liked to perform at least two acts which made him and Margaret, according to the California statutes, liable to fine or imprisonment or both—but his repertory was fixed. He was like the concertgoer who, preferring a steady fare of Beethoven and Brahms, has learned to like one Bartok concerto, and then let his taste freeze there. She wondered if she could forestall discoveries by Harry by intimating that she wanted to be led up fresh paths; he might think it a result of her having brooded on sex while he was away and take it as a tribute to what he'd aroused. But suppose he launched on different sorts of fun and, games from those she and Edwards played? It was always possible that Harry hadn't pushed out any further on the frontiers of sex with her because she had shown him as the wife of six months she'd been when he left for the South Pacific that she wasn't yet at ease with what he'd taught her to date. Maybe it would be better to tell him she'd read something interesting in a book—improving myself while you were away, dear.

So Margaret joked inwardly and quaked inwardly and pored over scruples and examined considerations, and was glad that matters were heading for a resolution. Then word came from Harry that his leave would be in Auckland. She blazed into anger at Harry — she was even angrier because she couldn't express her rage with him, to him. She wrote him about the Navy's unfairness, its arrogance, its brutal lack of consideration. She had to write the letter over because in one spot she wrote "you" instead of "the Navy;" as she read the completed letter, it seemed impossible to her that Harry wouldn't clearly see "you" everywhere in the letter instead of "the Navy," but she mailed it anyway. Harry was dense enough to miss anything, if he was dense enough not to have come home at all costs — desertion, mutiny — if he was dense enough not to recognize across the Pacific how ready she was for him. She had never wanted him so much, if only to match him against Edwards. She had been inflamed by that idea of randy homecoming.

She didn't believe he would spend a chaste leave in Auckland. He was a practical and predictable sort of man, who would consider himself to be behaving ridiculously if he didn't get laid while on leave; she had heard some injudicious stories about Auckland from friends of Harry's who'd had fine times there with Red Cross girls and the friendly natives. Now, no matter when it was that Harry came home, he wouldn't come back to her as the man deprived of sex, hungry as a stallion, about whom her thoughts had flickered so lecherously. She had been titillating herself with the idea of herself in bed with Harry; now occasionally she titillated herself with the idea of Harry in bed with another girl, and had her revenge on Harry by allowing these imaginings to heat up her fun in bed with Edwards.

While they had been waiting for Harry's return Edwards had made love to her more urgently and more often than ever before; presumably he too was inflamed by the notion of hungry Harry pleasuring himself in

The Duration

Margaret's bed. She had answered this ardor, but tenderly and in an absent-minded way as if over his shoulder she were looking for approaching Harry. Now in anger and frustration she flared up to match Edwards. She recognized too that Edwards' nerves were better, making him more certain of himself in bed; he mounted her in triumph because Harry couldn't, and she responded to the statement of satisfaction she felt in his muscles.

Edwards stood, naked, with his back to the bed where Margaret lay naked. He was thinking about what he intended to do. While he thought, he firmed up. He turned around and peacocked before he got into the bed and into Margaret.

Visions of pile drivers danced through his head; it occurred to him to celebrate himself. "I'm big, I'm hard," he exclaimed.

Antiphonally she replied, "Yes, yes—you're so big you're so hard." She was apt to overstate the implied comparison, in which Harry came off worse than was actually the case.

Edwards lay a hulk, a wreck. She hovered over him, white and shimmering as a shark; she watched, waiting, for signs of a sea change, then through tropic seas she sank and swirled about his mainmast. "Full fathom five," she cried.

[SIX]

Edwards didn't like being a civilian, and a young one, in wartime, but he didn't mind it as much as some men would have. He was better off than Lucius, a pacifist who when asleep sometimes dreamed of himself in splendid uniforms, a berserker's or conquistador's gene still existed, fuming, somewhere within. Awake, Lucius thanked god he was a civilian — though he tended to be a little vague about how it happened that he was one. Edwards wasn't sure if it was because of his age plus his children, or lf the *Observer* had obtained a deferment for him, or if Lucius' health really was as shaky as he maintained it was. In any case, Lucius' gratitude for his exemption was never very loud or very open; wartime, with all its poster warnings about careless talk, had the effect of aggravating his tendency to feel that someone was watching him as closely as Hook watched Peter for bad form, and that if he were caught in a lapse he would be fed to the crocodile; the years he had spent as a Newspaper Guild organizer had strengthened him in his view of the world as a conspiracy which must be propitiated, disliked and prudently resisted.

Lucius had an ingrained Great Plains dislike of militarism and an accurate apprehension of how lethal the clutch of blind discipline might be to him personally; but, caught in the vortex of his swirl of varying Spanish and Swedish currents, he dreamed recurrently and not unhappily that he had made his way into the Navy or Army Air Corps as an officer—but an impostor.

It seldom happened to Edwards that anyone tried to give him a bad time because he wasn't in uniform. He had a sturdy sense of his own fitness and rightness, which communicated itself to other people: a small man who is self-possessed but not self-assertive wins trust; think what Napoleon have been if he'd had Talleyrand's early advantages. Edwards was protected from sneers on the street, jeers from enlisted men whom the uniform galled, by the fact that he looked like a married man with at least two children. There also was something in his neatness, his air of reserve, his poise that suggested to these men that he might be an officer on leave: an Army officer. He was too four-square to be at home in anything floating. If he had been a hero, a stranger would feel instinctively, it must have been in the defense of a fixed point.

The only people who sometimes made Edwards uneasy in his civilian status were his father's male contemporaries. Edwards had been a double disappointment to his father. That gentleman and scholar of the law, as precise, as assured, as finely-drawn in blacks and whites and as unaware that he was about to become archaic as the steel engravings that illustrated Victorian books, was incapable of intentionally letting his only son see that a sickly boy was an embarrassment to him, who had set at Amherst track records that still endured. But something registered with the boy; maybe a remark heard through a half-open door, and then shot down and buried in an unmarked grave by the pickets of memory; or his father's slightly-too-high-pitched enjoyment of watching Edwards' healthy cousins play baseball, in summer on the San Mateo farm.

The child sensed what in later life he would have no trouble in retrospectively recognizing: that behind the reserve his father showed the world was a special layer of aloofness, exhibited only to his son, behind which lurked a strong man's anger at any weakling and a strong man's rage and self-doubt at having produced a flawed child, kept in check only by all the urbanity and natural goodness and equity of mind his father could summon up.

Perhaps too the boy realized, better than his father could — the law tends to give slight weight to the importance of motive — that the man's struggle with himself wasn't always successful. Who could say if the door was left open entirely by accident, if the praise given the cousin who hit a home run was spoken in utmost innocence of how it might exacerbate the boy on the sidelines? Maybe Edwards could. All children are Freudians; no child believes that any action of his elders is random; children look instinctively behind the explanation to the motive. Edwards, until he was in his teens, continued to revere and love his father; but insurrection was being readied, and like all rebellions against monarchy it aimed itself initially not at the king but at his court and his evil counselors. By the time he was nine Edwards was firmly set against becoming a lawyer.

Sometimes his mother, taking him with her on a shopping tour, would stop by for some reason at his father's law offices, where his father would greet them with a rendering in miniature of the pride and satisfaction with which a medieval English king might have greeted at court in London his vassals from the duchy of Normandy: each set of feudatories reinforcing his prestige with the other set. Though Edwards was heir apparent to one realm and heir presumptive to the other, the rebel within him who hadn't yet surfaced wasn't having any part of this; the office bored and oppressed him; he hated the sight and smell of law books, leather chairs and paneling; he got his head caught in an elevator door, for which his mother blamed his father, a sequence which the unseen rebel may have pondered. But when revolt showed itself it took the classic oblique pattern of assault upon the king's associates.

A partner in his father's firm, dining with the Edwards, asked the boy the ritual question whether he intended to follow his father's profession. "No, I want to be a newspaperman," said Edwards. This was news to his father, who came close to gaping and plainly was injured. It was the first time Edwards had known he could hurt his father; it made him feel guilty, but it was quite clear to the child that this sensation of power to do damage might be an alloyed pleasure but had instantly become a necessity to him. In a way his choice of career was news to Edwards, too. It was true that he wanted to be a newspaperman that week, but the week before he'd fancied himself as an architect, and last month as a naturalist. Still, his future was determined as he saw his father's resolve harden against this announced career, and his own will stiffened and forever embraced the trade of journalist.

The boy dimly realized he now held the advantage. From now on, it was up to him to say whether there was to be war—supposing that either party had the power to make this decision; probably this war, like most others, had a momentum of its own that couldn't be resisted. It wasn't beyond a child's perception to see that a mature man might feel ridiculous arguing with a nine-year-old over his choice of profession, or to recognize in his father apprehensions of guilt, a sense that he had failed his son, which might cause him to believe that he had forfeited what otherwise he would have regarded as his unquestioned right to legislate his son's life without granting his son the veto power.

John was now old enough to have dinner with his parents. At the dinner table his father began giving accounts of his day's work, seemingly addressed to his wife but actually carefully scaled to the child's comprehension — a fact which of course didn't escape the child's notice, the swaggering conceit of many children who have no brothers or sisters is partly due to their not realizing that nearly all children see through parents as easily as they do. One evening Edwards presented his parents with a newspaper he had produced, typed with two fingers on an old machine he had found in the attic. It contained stories about his father's cases. His mother appeared to enjoy these stories a good deal; sometimes in the evening, when the Edwards' were entertaining; she would come into John's bedroom, smelling of perfume and martinis, and ask to borrow the latest copy of his paper, to read to the guests. Edwards would sneak to the head of the staircase and hear his stories read aloud, to boozy laughter. He was not displeased; his conviction that adults mostly missed the point transferred itself for the duration of his life to people who read what others wrote.

Garrison Edwards stopped relating his days at table. He told himself that he had been making a fool of himself — which was true — and that he would influence

The Duration

John when he was older: seventeen, maybe; an age when a son could be companionable with his father, he thought. His own adolescence had been spent peacefully in an Eastern preparatory school; his skirmishes with his father, during vacations, seemed only the normal frictions between a host and a guest whose visit has run too long. He could remember once listening to his father's advice when he was seventeen; it had been about the handling of a difficult horse it had been good, and he had followed it; he persuaded himself that this must have happened often.

He was completely unprepared for the monstrous transformation of his son John into a thirteen-year-old boy. He stared, repelled; he shouted for help. He was not a querulous man and he seldom complained about the world or its treatment of him to his wife; he was apt in fact, to behave as if he were his own client and his thoughts were privileged matter which he was honor-bound not to disclose to her. If he was querulous now, it was not only because he felt the unfair leverage that every sickly child wields, but also because he dimly sensed that his son's illness had robbed him of an unusual opportunity to possess the mistress-companion which is what most men want their wife to be most of the time.

It wasn't an era when motherhood won you many points, either self-awarded or from others. Louise Edwards was as determined as anyone in the 1920s to have a good time, and to be as unencumbered as possible. Marriage had made possible her semi-escape from her own mother, a forceful matron of the Spanish California baronial strain, whose own parents went back far enough to have been born just too late to be able to remember Mexican California. Louise's mother cherished many Castilian ideals and precepts—not as ways to behave that had virtue because they were specifically Castilian (the Sanhuidos, unlike some of the great ranch-owning families, who still held land in Spain, long ago had cut nearly all ties with their ancestral nation), but simply as ways to behave that had virtue. You could see the Spanish heritage in Louise's looks—tall, elegant, meant for a mantilla.

The flapper fashions shouldn't have suited her, but they oddly did, giving an edge to her sexual attractiveness, which was considerable. The short, flimsy, straight-hanging dresses gave her a saucy look of a girl sitting around in her slip in the parlor of a whorehouse, waiting to be taken upstairs by a customer whose taste ran to the dignified kind, Prohibition gin (the Edwards' bootlegger was named Thackeray, and was addressed as Mr. Thackeray, with the deference accorded a tradesman whose services one fears to lose) with its terrible wallop suited Louise too. Two glasses, and she began looking sideways out of the elegant eyes. The female equivalent of the thin man who lives inside every fat man is the small, flirtatious woman who inhabits so many high, stately women; but Louise's small flirtatious self had something frightening about it, like trolls or sexy fawns, as if it had the power to change into still another shape—this one a woman who would have the pants off the man to whom she was talking in no time: scare them off him, most likely. Possibly the real reason the fashions of the time sat well on Louise was because they forced on her an ambiguity of appearance which perfectly expressed her mocking, elusive, complex nature.

Louise hadn't meant to get greatly involved with her children. She had intended to have them brought up, until they were of school age, by a governess, who would see that they were well cared for, were a credit to their parents, and generally speaking got a good start in life, Louise intended to be fond of them, and believed they would be fond of her. But John turned out to be an only child; he was followed by two miscarriages, and a ban on further pregnancies.

She almost lost John, too. He came home from a day at the beach with a sore throat which turned into rheumatic fever. His temperature rose to a hundred and six; his life hung in balance for a night, and was saved only by a young doctor who was willing to take a chance on an untried drug. Louise discovered that her notion of motherhood was completely inadequate to contain what motherhood was; it was like trying to run the Mississippi through a Dutch canal. She developed a tigress' heart, though she kept it wrapped in a player's hide. So she listened without much sympathy to Garrison's complaints of their son, and said in a somewhat sardonic voice that she'd see what she could do about it. It didn't help Garrison's case that this was the time of the stock market collapse, which badly hurt the Edwards financially. Shocked out of his taciturnity, Garrison railed to Louise against a good many people and institutions, and against the time, his tone bewildered and indignant. When he switched to John she heard him out, but with a strong female sense that whatever he said could be discounted, since he obviously had lost his grip and failed in at least one of his prime male functions.

In high school John began using Farragut Edwards as his byline in the school newspaper. Farragut, his middle name, was a family name—his mother's family—running back to the 1850s when the admiral had been commandant of the Mare Island naval yard, and had made an agreeable impression upon the Spanish Californians. Its employment was sheer romanticism on

John's part, jettisoned by the time he was out of college, when he became John again (what his name was, for byline purposes, wouldn't have mattered much at the *Observer*, where bylines were awarded sparingly; Edwards had worked there almost two years before he was given one). But his choice of a writing name appeared conceived in malice to Garrison, who had talked Louise out of giving the child Farragut as a Christian name on the ground that it was too much to inflict on the boy. Whatever resentment Garrison felt over this he had to conceal — he couldn't very well complain to Louise, whose sympathy he was invoking, that the boy was using the name she had tried to give him. But Garrison soon had plenty of opportunity to let loose at his son, as hostilities moved into a new arena.

The family quarrel as an American institution flourished at its height between 1933 and 1941, during the peacetime administrations of Franklin Roosevelt. Sophocles and Marx and Freud and St. Augustine and Joyce collaborating couldn't have done justice to the scenes that went on between parents and their children. These were made worse by the circumstance that in those lean days most families were lucky to have even one car (which was what the Edwards had); the young were rendered even less tolerant of their elders than in later decades by the painful fact that they couldn't escape them by roaring off into the night where they had something better to do. The final ingredient necessary to produce a witches' brew — timing — was not lacking.

The President's fireside chats on the radio came when many people were at the dinner table. Stomachs knotted, brows churned even before the salutation was spoken: "My friends..." In the magisterial pause which followed this greeting the first shot would be fired. In

[79]

many households it took the form of an imitation (of varying quality) by the head of the household, of the words just orotundly uttered. Garrison's style was a little subtler than that. He would comment unfavorably on the impression the President, were he an attorney about to open a case, would make on a jury — on any but the meanest and least intelligent sort of jury.

"No wonder the man never practiced," he would add. A variant was: "He never practiced, you know." He was perfectly aware that he had said this often before. His aim was to annoy; his lawyer's instinct was to abrade any irritated surface that showed upon an opponent. Sometimes his son became angry enough to say hard things about lawyers generally. His father was hurt then; they all (Louise too) became abashed; all three knew this quarrel wasn't about Roosevelt, but sprang from much deeper oppositions riving their family structure. None of them wanted this to come out in the open; after a pause, they fled back to politics. Across the nation people were carefully concealing from themselves what they were arguing about: parents, declaiming against the opinions and behavior of their children and especially their partisanship of Roosevelt's subversive doctrines, were railing at their own parents as personified by the massive, righteous, self-contained, impervious figure of the President.

There was something unfair about him: they recognized it very well. He had unfair advantages (being rich, being President) as their own parents had held unfair advantages - being older, being parents, they knew, now, how much hypocrisy had lurked within their parents' posture; Roosevelt inevitably must be a hypocrite. They grew purple at their children who, refusing to admit the double-dealing nature of Franklin Roosevelt, without knowing it were denying the validity of the case their elders had spent a lifetime building up against their elders.

Louise generally entered these arguments on John's side; but she was an uncertain element, like the Stanleys at Bosworth Field, with her own reasons for doing mischief to everybody. Sometimes she attacked Roosevelt, to placate her husband or to annoy her son, who, she often felt these days needed trimming down to size; about three feet high would suit her perfectly. Also, she didn't like the President. He reminded her of her mother. (She he read that *he* had a dominating mother, but this confused her, so she forgot it and never thought about it again.)

Garrison, held at arm's length by his son held at fingertips' length by his wife, increasingly turned to his male contemporaries. He became a clubman. None of his distinguished coevals (Garrison and most of his friends were about of an age with Roosevelt) was puerile enough to say, few of them were puerile enough even to think, that the President certainly would have been blackballed if he had applied to join any of their clubs, but it was pleasant for them *to feel,* not to think that this was so. When they came to dinner with the Edwards and the political argument began Garrison appealed, implicitly or openly for his friends' support but rarely got it.

Garrison was a little too near to being flawless even for his friends, who had all sorts of high standards. They didn't mind at all that he had a flawed son—physically flawed, presumably flawed in character. They were pleased, by their genial tolerance of John's youthfully liberal views, to imply that no meals were bloodied, no ulcers nourished, no Atreide conflicts fought on this theme (they were lying outrageously) at their own dinner tables.

The Duration

The coming of war altered the direction of a good many fields of force. By then John and his father had reached an armistice. As John's health grew better his mother showed less concern over it. More accurately, she devoted about as much attention to it as ever, but it was becoming apparent that John's constitution was an increasingly poor field for the investment of emotion, and was yielding her steadily diminishing returns. Garrison could dismiss her worrying over John as annoying silliness, not as a declaration that the vital interest of her life lay elsewhere than with himself. His son plainly had settled down to a newspaper career; he had his own apartment; he had his own life, which contained no elements of which his parents could out and out disapprove. His maternal grandmother had died and left him a small income; this helped a great deal. His parents were not obliged to apologize for him or to despise him because he was poor.

Furthermore, though he had done nothing to earn or wheedle this legacy, his parents respected him for having gotten some money out of the old woman. She had been generous to them in her will, but they always had known they could count on her to be correct; to Edwards she had been a little more than correct, and it impressed them.

Edwards was in no hurry to marry. Family life hadn't entirely recommended itself to him; though he never said so, even to himself; he accepted it that he would marry. In his relationships with girls he was aggressive, persistent and cautious — like a gopher; like a gopher he was always very conscious of his refuge. Not many girls got into his apartment. Some thought he was lavish, because of the expensive places he took them to on weekends; some thought he was cheap, because he laid them, or tried to lay then, in his car's back seat or a

Peninsula field. Those who went out with him for any extended time realized they were being steered away from his apartment, and fought to obtain entrance - some even believed that he had another girl or an undisclosed wife, stashed away in there.

Once they began to press him in earnest to see his quarters, he let them in at once; they were always disappointed; it was just like any bachelor's apartment. If the girl was sleeping with him, he had her, in his unmade bed. If she wasn't, he encouraged her to cook a meal for him, which she couldn't do without washing all those dishes in the sink. He might have gone on in this way indefinitely; but the war came.

Soon after Pearl Harbor he realized that his father's friends were being short with him. He might turn up at his parents' for dinner and find his father in the library, over drinks with a contemporary. The other man would shake hands with John, fail to inquire about his doings these days, and turn back to Garrison with a story of what his own son was up to in the New Hebrides. Garrison was long beyond embarrassment over what he couldn't help feeling were his son's shortcomings; but he was gentle and sensitive in many ways, and he was embarrassed on John's behalf. He would try to draw John into the conversation; the other man would switch to the subject of his own grandchildren.

Edwards told himself there was nothing personal in their malice; it was only the old instinct to shrug off the company of the unfit when danger is around. Also, after you have heard about it for twenty years, the ill health of other people's children becomes a bore: it's difficult not to feel there's some element of fraud in it, especially if the child, grown, looks as healthy as Edwards did. (Every branch of the armed forces had rejected Edwards, nevertheless; they appeared to worry less about his fitness than about the possibility that he would become a future charge upon the government; perhaps they felt a little mean about this, which may have been why the Army Air Corps examiner reported with such a note of triumph that Edwards was also slightly color-blind.)

Still, it was hard to bear the slights of those rich, crafty, well-tailored, whiskey-throated old men, some of whom he admired and would have liked to model himself upon, with some streamlining. Any male civilian younger than fifty, whatever his condition, feels lonely in wartime. But there is available to him one profound comfort which is seldom open either to censorious old men or to young men in uniform — the constant company of a pretty girl. Of course Edwards didn't fall in love with Margaret and induce her to fall in love with him, just to prove his virility to his father's friends, or to get back at the men of his age who sometimes passed him, with unsmiling looks in the street. But he was marvelously ready for her.

[SEVEN]

They met at a cocktail party, one of those wartime cocktail parties at which all the guests were as spirited, not to say frenzied, and as uneasy as if their host had been Hieronymous Bosch. The invitations might as well have read: bring your own discomfort. Some women felt displeased because there weren't enough men at the parties, others because there were too many women; and both of these grounds for complaint imposed themselves as floating, surface annoyances, quite separate from the greater deprivation of not having a man which most of the younger women were undergoing. The young wives felt that they were camels who just might not be able to bear this extra straw they felt that they were married not to a man, but to the war: war was their husband, and the bastard was too mean-minded even to allow them a party flirtation. Nearly all the women young and old were gripped by sadness and apprehension. The parties were Babylonian; but the message

Belshazzar got was delivered in style; he didn't come home at the end of the evening and find it lying on his doorstep in a little yellow envelope; furthermore it was forthright and didn't open with regrets. A communal shame possessed the young wives. They behaved as if they had come to the parties straight from a jail where they had not been allowed to bathe: they were afraid they smelled of their solitary cells, and they made sad jailhouse jokes to one another. The civilian men of course were used to being uncomfortable; but at a party, in the same room with men in uniform they didn't know or didn't know very well, they were as badly off as citizens of an occupied country. (They could hardly wait for the war to be over so that they could rush into the movie houses and sit entranced watching films glorifying Rommel, in which our side took a good pasting, or won in an unsympathetic manner.)

As for the men who were back from the theaters of war, they seemed avid enough for pleasures and party-going, but they too tended to huddle together in the camaraderie of a shared unease: the place they had come from was not jail but a hospital, (sometimes, of course, this was literally true). Like those who have reappeared in the world after an illness, they nearly always looked healthier and less marked by their experience than people had expected, but intermittently they displayed the convalescent's sense of having been displaced in time, his irritation with people who have stayed foolishly well and so know nothing, his preference for the company of those who have shared or attended on his fever dreams, humiliations, fears and symptoms. (To the dead, probably, death seems the only way to be and ghosts when they manifest themselves are only expressing uncontrollable irritation with the living who refuse to understand this.)

[86]

The Duration

The men in uniform who seemed most at ease were the officers who worked at desks in the downtown office buildings the Army and Navy had taken over. (One of those buildings had been a spectacularly unsuccessful twenty-five-story hotel. Edwards thought the severe young armed sentries who stood at its doors were an unimaginative measure. The Navy, he told Lucius, should have rounded up all the doormen who used to fawn on the infrequent arrivals at that hotel, made them petty officers and put them in charge of keeping people out.) The desk officers had their own courage; they shook hands with the fighting men and chatted as smoothly as if barbed words like "Twelfth Naval District Commando" were vulgarities they'd never heard of.

Their manner lay somewhere between the assurance of a man who reads all the files and hears what the admiral has to say about them, and the bravado of a man who's been in a nasty scandal but meets his acquaintances unruffled, patronizing them a little if they falter into some oblique mention of his trouble. Of all the partygoers those who were most comfortable with themselves were the businessmen who were making money out of the war. Their self-possessed flesh was by Jan van Eyck, who as he painted them had murmured softly to them that the pretty young wives worked for them now and the fighting men would have to come to them for jobs after the war. At their parties you had the best chance of getting something close to decent liquor. The drinks at most of the parties were terrible.

People drank manhattans — those were the last years of the manhattan; its sweetness killed the taste of the raw whiskey — or Southern drinks which must have been the cough syrup that Scarlett O'Hara swigged by the quart in her old age when she was trying to hide the fact that she'd become a lush. But one magnate, who knew Edwards' father, took Edwards from a cocktail-party into a private little room where he unlocked a cabinet and took out a bottle of brandy that had been given to him by an exiled king, who was cultivating American businessmen while he sweated out the war in Kensington Gardens. It was wonderful brandy; Edwards was offered a small shot of it, and another because his appreciation of it was flattering. After he had drunk it Edwards remembered that Dr. Johnson had said that brandy is for heroes.

One day in the summer of 1942 Edwards went on assignment to Letterman Hospital, where the first wounded from Guadalcanal had arrived. They looked tanned and healthy, and were cheerful, though many had an arm or a leg missing. But a boy about twenty who had lost a leg said to Edwards: "What am I gonna do without a leg, you tell me that? What am I gonna do?" He could have been the kind of adolescent who stood on his two legs on street corners Saturday night, simmering a grievance against everybody who was better off than him, but he had a grievance now and Edwards couldn't think of anything helpful to say to him. Edwards went back to the office and wrote a story, as underplayed and effective as he knew how to make it, which allowed him to feel better: artful handling of the plight of the limbless brought in its train a comforting sensation that limblessness was crass and excessive, a state which he had kindly smoothed over for those men, as if they had spelled it wrong.

Edwards was not Celtic and not anecdotal and wasn't really much of a writer as a child and as a man he never had been deprived of anything vital; for any or all of these reasons he felt no need to keep reworking his

material, and so he didn't mention the wounded men
from Guadalcanal to the girl he met that evening at a
cocktail party. She was black-haired, blue-eyed, lightly
coated with freckles and amused assurance; her short
fresh mouth, turned up at the corners, had the shape of
the deadly Turkish bow.

The party was in an apartment, which had been created on the top floor of one of the Presidio Heights
town houses, three and four stories high, built in the
1920s at the latest, which line the blocks that dead-end
into the Presidio wall. The presence just over the wall of
the rough untamed growth, trees and shrubs of the
Presidio gives the houses a pleasant air of being on the
edge of a forest; if you came out of a party in one of
those houses and found a man heisting your hubcaps,
he might be wearing Lincoln green. The trees and the
absence of through traffic and perhaps a sense of being
bordered by a secure entity—a stone wall, the Army,
history—give those short blocks a considerable sereni-
ty. A man who lived down the block from the house
where the party was, who didn't look like a sensitive
man, had been moved to buy a silvery little bell for his
Bentley, to sound instead of its horn.

The apartment on the top floor had been servants'
bedrooms. They would have had to climb a steep wood-
en staircase at the back of the house, instead of the
broad shallow stairway which now ran up the building's exterior, and their windows would have been
small and small-paned, so probably they regarded the
view as no more of a privilege than if it had been the
wall of an air shaft; but the windows were large now,
and the great splendid sweeping scene of the Gate and
the Marin County hills, with the nervous bay in so
glassily good a mood that it might have achieved temporary rapport with a flock of swans—the scene, at this

twilight hour, had a quieting effect on the party guests, who turned to it and deferred to it and even yearned toward it, as if it were music to which they knew they ought to be listening and which they even wanted to listen to, if they'd only had the time. The ceilings, directly under the roof of the old house, sloped sharply and with unexpected angles and projections. The shadows they created, and the dimness of the lights, kept subdued not to detract from the view, made it difficult for Edwards to interpret the glimmers and shades in the face of the Irish girl. She had made some sort of quick acceptance of him; she was welcoming him to something, but he couldn't be sure what.

Everyone at the party was young, and the shadowy room throbbed with possibilities. Most of the girls were married, but few were with their husbands; some had come with other men; some, like Edwards' new friend Elizabeth had brought another girl. There were enough unattached men in uniform, single men or men whose wives were at home somewhere else in the country, to strike a balance. It was summer, and although San Francisco's summers are conducted under gray skies which concede nothing to the season, intimations of warmth had drifted in from the suburbs, like rumors of victory. The partygoers, young, felt the languorousness of the season, which seemed to advise them that much was permissible; relaxing in the flow of summer, they were swept back to the summers of three or four years ago, when they had been pairing off. It was happening again, but with a deeper, wilder excitement now, because the experience toward which they were moving was adultery. It seemed — they were surprised that they'd never realized it before; *how long has this been going on?* was the melody to which those girls moved — it seemed inevitable, a last step toward adulthood. They

had found themselves, at every move toward independence, harassed by their elders; but in this final grasping
of initiative, which might be expected to stir up the
fiercest resistance they'd yet encountered from among
the older generation, the young felt themselves privileged.

The fire they were putting out, which the elders
could only watch while the young got burned gave
them a lot of license. They hated the war; it wasn't a
shining cause to them, just an intolerable interruption;
but deep in them was a usually unrecognized satisfaction at being part of an event of an historical and personal magnitude such as the generations preceding
them hadn't known, couldn't advise them about or
patronize them over in light of senior experience. The
bitter ones called it *your war* to their parents, but it was
their war and later they would cherish it. In the meantime they were content to imply that the weight of so
much history bearing down on them made them absent-
mindedly licentious—that they went to bed with one
another as their elders (with their fewer responsibilities) might, while playing a difficult bridge hand, scoop
up and gobble whole handfuls of candy.

Most of the people at the party knew most of the
others. Elizabeth knew hardly anybody. Her husband
overseas, she explained to Edwards, had been a college
buddy of their host, who occasionally asked her to parties out of a sense of duty or the wish to keep an eye on
her. She let fall this last observation with perfect ease,
intimating that she was too seasoned not to acknowledge the possibility of her misbehavior and too urbane
to give Edwards a hint of whether her husband's friend
was right to doubt her. She spoiled the effect a little,
when Edwards smiled his admiration of her finesse into
her martini-flushed eyes, by smiling back as broadly as

an Eliza Doolittle who has brought it off. The blonde girl who had come with Elizabeth didn't know anybody, Edwards gathered that she and Elizabeth weren't old acquaintances; in this wartime city where people swirled around one another and floated into new combinations and then were swept away, the two girls had struck up an alliance in a quick recognition that they were effective foils for one another.

It wasn't just a matter of dark and light; they complemented one another as England and Ireland might have if the Normans had conquered Ireland first and England second. Margaret was larger, quieter, milder, possessed a greater quantity of conventional beauty, was more cultivated and gave off a reassuring sense of being close to the mainland, and would be the first choice of fairies who nevertheless would find themselves better received by the other realm. She was the norm from which Elizabeth could spin away, as a girl dances away from her partner whose stillness heightens the sense of her motion, or to which Elizabeth could retreat with her eyebrows raised at a man: how could anyone have misunderstood a nice girl, the close friend of so surpassingly nice a girl as Margaret, so incredibly as to make her such a suggestion? But being a norm has its satisfactions.

Elizabeth was pretty because she was determined to be, but Margaret was almost beautiful without trying. Certainly she wasn't unaware of her endowment. She was a tall slender girl but she had a fine deep chest which she seemed to savor with each breath she took; if Venus of Melos breathed, she would breathe like Margaret. She moved with a slow grace that seemed to contain some calculation; one imagines that Venus arranged those draperies herself. Other men seemed to have been quicker than Edwards to estimate and esteem these attractions. Men were gathered about the pair of girls, but there seemed to be a growing sentiment in favor of Margaret. Then, as the tide of drinks rose, Margaret rose with it, like a boat coming into its element. Her quietness dropped from her like a veil from an Arab girl, like everything from a stripper, Edwards realized he had failed to recognize a born life/belle of the party/ball; the kind of girl dear old dad proposed to, and was turned down, before he married the girl that sonny in the song wants one like.

The circle closed in on her, and gradually Elizabeth was edged out, into a corner with Edwards. Her manner suggested that it was exactly what she wanted. This may have been partly true; she seemed to enjoy mischievous suggestion, which is most safely and most effectively practiced on one man at a time; she told him proudly that her father had been a captain in the IRA in the Time of Troubles, and evidently she had inherited a taste for significant conversations in dark corners. But she couldn't be expected to relish Margaret's success; Edwards resented it himself, on Elizabeth's behalf and his own. His first deep impression of Margaret, irrational though it was, was that she had shut him out. He suggested to Elizabeth that she have dinner with him, and she agreed, though by now she was so irritated with Margaret that she failed to show much enthusiasm. Shrugging in Margaret's direction, she said, "It'll be hours before she's ready to eat," implying that the trouble with Margaret was, not that she was too attractive to men, but that she drank too much. Edwards could see this wasn't true; obviously Margaret's long fine legs were hollow, both of them. He took Elizabeth out, increasingly frequently, in the next few weeks. He had been right: she had a taste for intrigue; but she was a double agent. He couldn't tell if she was on her husband's side or his; or if she didn't know but enjoyed the confusion; or if she did know but was so fundamentally attuned to complexity that she would always if possible avoid ultimate commitment; or if she did know but was making a good thing out of both sides. She gladly, even eagerly, accorded him all the shows and panoply of sexual love, and most of its minor privileges. Everyone thought they were sleeping together. She hardly could take a step without clinging to his arm.

At parties if he told a dirty story she laughed knowingly, as if she had twenty times as much reason to be knowing as anyone else listening to him; in bars, she sat pressed against him in booths, her arm resting on his arm or thigh. In private they necked like super-adolescents, with an extra dimension of desperation. She would telephone him at the office to tell him a dirty story she'd just heard, as if she were so devoted to him that to keep even this by-product of sex from him for a few hours would make her feel unfaithful. (They dealt so much in sexy jokes as an offset to their not having any real sex together; he tried to rape her, and she willingly offered herself for rape, in the medium of words.)

They had long, caressingly intimate telephone talks late at night. She cooked for him; she was willing to do anything for him, except to be willing. He knew he was being used; just as surely as Elizabeth wasn't being had, he was, Elizabeth couldn't live without the warmth of a man, but wanted it at bargain rates. He continued to take her out because she was very entertaining and there were other girls to at least take the edge off him and naturally he hoped that some night she would lose her self-control or get tired of it. Sometimes, when she met him in the evening after work, Margaret would be with her and they'd all have a drink.

The Duration

Margaret was easy and friendly and open with him, but it worried him a little that there never was anything knowing in her manner. Of course it wasn't in her style to drop flattering hints that she knew what the two of them were up to; still, he supposed her utter acceptance of the situation must mean that she knew they weren't up to anything, really, and probably despised him a little for it. Or maybe, he further worried, she did think he was sleeping with Elizabeth, and her easiness with him was a buffer, behind which she was disapproving him. He didn't think it remarkable that he wanted Margaret to think well of him: he'd noticed that everyone did. Sometimes, in the relaxed way of the times, as they sat drinking in the Patent Leather Room or the Mark's lower bar, they would acquire a strange but presentable man in uniform for Margaret and the four of them would go on to dinner together.

As the couples parted, at evening's end, the men would exchange over the girls' heads a look of complicity and mutual congratulation: Edwards because his pride required that he pretend he was going to get what he knew he wasn't going to get, and the other man because he thought he was going to get what apparently he never did get since Margaret never was seen again with these chance escorts.

Other evenings, Margaret would leave them after a couple of drinks, declining to stay longer; she showed neither envy or reprobation of them, but walked gravely away, seeming perfectly content to be going alone wherever she was going. Her walk was good to watch; sometimes, as she left them, Edwards looked after her with what he hoped was an academic lust, much as one will sometimes feel while studying some desirable aspect of a woman one doesn't want. Elizabeth also, more bleakly, studied Margaret as she left then.

Edwards gradually had realized that Elizabeth had latched on to Margaret out of a conviction that Margaret could be a friend who would fill all kinds of needs, large and small, in Elizabeth's deprived wartime existence; and that she never had been able to forgive Margaret for the strength with which she had felt and still felt this conviction. Did she unwillingly suspect herself of a sexual attachment to Margaret? He discounted most of what she had to say about Margaret; he wished she wouldn't talk about Margaret: her unease with the subject made him uneasy. But he was startled one evening as he stood baffled and panting before Elizabeth while she lay half-sprawled, not too happy herself, in the big armchair in his living room. She said, over the rough fast intervals of her breathing her voice ran smooth with mischief and malice and even true tender concern for poor lustful Edwards. "Why don't you try Margaret? I think she likes you."

He was truly startled. He'd come to think of Margaret as Elizabeth's friend—that woman friend with whom every man involved in a sexual relationship with a woman, marriage or not, finds he has to deal. The friend may be as heterosexual as Theodora, but toward the man who is sleeping with *her* friend (or trying to) she is curiously censorious; the disapproval may be masked by camaraderie, but behind the easy acceptance lurks the assumption that he is taking advantage of the woman he sleeps with and probably wants to take advantage of the friend, too. At best the friend shows herself, to the man as companionable as a jolly lesbian, at worst as hostile as an unjolly lesbian. Her aura is that of a fairly broadminded Victorian lady who finds herself dining alone with an Oriental potentate, whom she doesn't want to offend (if possible) for the sake of the Queen: warnings not to try anything curl

[96]

from her like the lazy smoke from the funnels of Her Majesty's warships, lying offshore peaceably but with emphasis.

Edwards now and then was sorry that it wasn't Margaret he had found himself with in a corner, at that party, but he knew a man sometimes has the bad luck to meet, first the wrong one for him of a pair of pretty women, and finds the other's door always closed against him, or at best opened rather condescendingly. He had never been unaware of Margaret's sexual tug upon him — to have ignored it, since it so obviously operated upon almost every man she met, would have been a peevish admission of his own insufficiency to deal with so full-blooded a girl, the sort of behavior that might be expected from the dehydrated bachelor Edwards was in danger of becoming, ten years from now. (Perhaps he was moving already in that direction; the fact that he'd allowed Elizabeth to put him off for so long, even though he discharged himself upon other girls, might argue a certain weariness with the campaigns of sex, a willingness to conduct them in the reasonable eighteenth century manner, battling for the sake of appearances and without too much exertion.) But he came so slowly to a full realization of how desirable a girl Margaret was that it must have been a recognition against which he fought.

He had accepted inaccessibility, in the circumstances of his involvement with Elizabeth, but he was beginning to suspect that he found Margaret a good deal more attractive than was comfortable for him to live with. There is no cure for true inaccessibility in a woman except to dislike her, or to make friends with her, which permits a soothing brotherly sexiness of relationship. Edwards couldn't try to make friends with Margaret, because she was Elizabeth's friend, and

[97]

would be sure to misinterpret his approaches (or interpret them correctly); and he felt it was safer to keep her
at a distance. (If he was developing a yen for her, he certainly didn't want either her or Elizabeth to notice it.
They might joke about it. In fact, he learned later, they
did.)

He fed himself small regular doses of dislike for
her; in the pattern into which they had fallen—man,
woman and woman's woman friend—it was normal for
him to be hostile to Margaret. In these ways he succeeded in inoculating himself against her as he viewed her
ordinarily, in street clothes or a cocktail frock, but he
wasn't proof against the sudden insights into one's real
attitudes provided by the jolt of novelty sometimes a
sweep of lust took him by surprise when he saw her in
some setting or dressed in some way which made her
unfamiliar to him, it didn't require the obvious titillations, appraising her for the first time in swim suit or
evening gown, to produce this pang: it was enough to
run into her outdoors at a party on somebody's lawn in
Burlingame, in a white linen summer dress, a white
straw hat on her long blonde hair, inclining her face to
sip from a full martini glass, then throwing her head
back with enjoyment as the glow ran down her throat.
He was helped, each time something like this happened, in thriving down and toning down and eventu-
ally dismissing for the day his perception of her sexual
attractiveness, by his belief that no other man, at the
moment, had the run of her.

It was time that after a few drinks, at parties, her
manner began to suggest more and more outrageously
that she was available, but Edwards guessed that slightly overheated flirtatiousness always had been her style.
He didn't think she was a tease—if you didn't count the
impulse to tease hurtingly which occasionally breaks

surface in every pretty woman; Lord Acton, if he had thought much about women, might have produced several other memorable dicta on the effects of power. On the contrary, Edwards believed that Margaret was warm-hearted and enjoyed making a man feel that, if the stars had been in the right conjunction that night and if only the guy hadn't been married or hadn't been a friend of Harry's or hadn't been Margaret's best friend's brother or hadn't suffered from some other disabling characteristic, he might have scored. But he also thought her behavior was significant—that, like so many of the war wives, she felt a necessity to mime out the sex she didn't permit herself to have. Quite literally, she went through all the motions, except the ultimate ones. It was easy for him to recognize this in Margaret because Elizabeth was an extreme case of the same thing.

On a Friday evening early that fall Edwards was walking up Post Street when he saw Margaret standing before the window of a department store, looking into it. Downtown San Francisco, almost any weekday evening around five-thirty, the air brisk and the early dark coming down over the civilized old buildings, has the air of a place not very far off from a party, to which everyone is hurrying, all the women seem to be carrying packages—the old women, one feels, have bought something for their grandchildren; the middle-aged ones have bought something for their children or even for their husbands; the young ones have bought something dashing to wear to bed, which they won't wear for more than ten minutes, that night.

Margaret had no packages and no air of having anywhere to go. Edwards wondered what in the window was holding her attention, but decided as he came closer, from her tranced air, that she wasn't seeing the window at all. He was going to stop to speak to her then decided it would be an intrusion. Just as he came level with her, she turned around. Sadly and acceptingly, she looked at him with a complete lack of surprise. They went to a bar, where they stayed until nearly ten o'clock, talking excitedly and telling each other that after one more drink they would go and have dinner.

"I never knew that you drink scotch," she said with the greatest possible interest. "I've seen you at so many parties and I never noticed you drank scotch. She put her hands around her glass on the bar and turned it, while she reflected; her head was inclined so that her blonde hair fell as a shield between her and Edwards. She raised her face to him. "You've got to understand that I love my husband," she said.

The front door of her apartment house was as far as he went that night, standing in the doorway of the shabby little building, exposed to the disapproval or prurience of passersby, they kissed desperately and rather drunkenly, but in the end she sent him away. "I'm not ready, John," she said. "You've got to woo me."

The wooing took six weeks. He was dogged about it, but he soon lost all certainty of whether he was making any progress. He had some experience of women's vagaries, but emotion had seized the reins from him and instead of waiting calmly with a huntsman's confidence, when she ducked into cover, he panicked and rode hallooing after her. She asked to see his apartment, warning him not to read too much into her request; but when they were there she invaded his bedroom boldly and, smiling wickedly, leaned on the bed and tested the springs.

Two days later he received a long, rambling letter, written at four in the morning, which asked what sort of girl she thought he was — she, who was fastidious about the language, actually used that phrase; he would have laughed if he hadn't been so upset. The letter said she wouldn't see him again. Next day she telephoned him cheerfully and said there was a party that night she wanted him to escort her to. To feel at sea and tossed about were unusual sensations to him; but he was in love, knew he was in love, had admitted to her and professed to her that he was in love, and he persevered.

When, finally, she let him make love to her she refused on the first night to take off her clothes. That was in his apartment. It soon dawned on them as her clothes came off and things went generally well that their lovemaking would have to be transferred to her apartment, though she had scruples about this — that apartment was a place she had been saving for Harry's enjoyment; it seemed to her that something should be reserved for Harry. But she couldn't, as a married woman, afford to have it become known that she spent whole nights, or most of them, away from her apartment — and it would become known; some friend of Harry's would arrive in town and call her from a bar up until midnight, or later after the bars closed and not find her home, three nights running; or her mother, who used the telephone as casually and in as quick response to impulse as she used her vocal chords, might call her at three in the morning from San Diego.

In her apartment, further scruples developed. The first night, they made love on her living room sofa — only less uncomfortable than the floor, which they also tried. But two nights later she took him by the hand and led him into her bedroom where she was magnificently lascivious. Of course, it wasn't Harry's bed she was taking him into — Harry never had occupied it, though he might in the future. In a way that made her betrayal worse; she had let him use Harry's bed before Harry had used it. He thought she felt the force of this, and meant him to feel it. Having embarked on adultery, she meant to enjoy it down to the last frisson. She was never a half-hearted girl.

Elizabeth was shocked. She avoided them. Once, at dusk, they ran into her on Grant Avenue, she released a hello and skittered off into a side street. She seemed to have grown thin and pinched. Next time they saw her was six months later, in the Patent Leather Room. They had sat down at a table before they noticed her at one of the huge leather-backed booths at the rear of the room. She sat sprawlingly. With her was a man in uniform, whom she caressed frequently. Her glance passed over Edwards and Margaret vaguely, triumphantly, with only a flicker of recognition. Edwards remembered that she had made a show of herself in public with him, but he decided she was sleeping with this man. Beside him he felt Margaret reaching the same conclusion. They smiled at one another and speculated on whether the man was her husband, and decided he was. It was that air of victorious respectability as she lounged there lewdly in the giant booth, inviting the world to see what she was willing to do for a man.

[EIGHT]

Tom Farrell, the night rewrite man, quit to take a job as public relations man for one of the Catholic universities in the Bay Area. His wife, through miscalculation, had had a fifth child. Mrs. Farrell of course favored the change of job, but so did Farrell, and not just because of the money. It wasn't only that he was tired of guiltily drinking in Malloy's, on the cuff, and of borrowing a dollar until payday, he was tired of Malloy's, and of himself in Malloy's, and of the griminesses and pettinesses and hypocrisies of his workday life. He was tired of having hell raised with him by the white-haired editorial bookkeeper because he'd taken a dollar-twenty-five cab instead of a streetcar, to get back from an assignment soon enough not to get dark looks from the desk.

The bookkeeper had passed beyond the common-place state of emotional identification with his employer's money, which for decades he had doted upon and doled out as if it were his own; he had transcended this garden variety of the vicarious enjoyment of wealth and had attained an exaltation of penuriousness, a nearly spiritual dedication to the cause of saving pennies for the spendthrift monarch he served. The bookkeeper's devotion merited a better faith to grow old for, a more awful Chief: he deserved at least the dignity of those Zulu impis which marched off the cliff at the king's command.

Farrell also was tired of the Chief's editorials calling in capital letters upon the government to place at least ninety per cent of the nation's war materiel at the disposal of General MacArthur, and he was tired of I love America Day, an observance invented by the Chief and dutifully noted by public officials, with the issuance of suitable proclamations, in all the cities where the Chief's papers were published. Farrell had written for two years the series of twenty or so stories which noted the approach and arrival of I love America Day, and chronicled its observance, in prose which was expected to grow more florid as the day approached, and to explode orgiastically when it arrived. Possibly the formula according to which these stories were written was derived from stories the Chief himself had written, generations ago when he devised this observance, for the stories unmistakably contained a note of triumph: the Chief had invented a holiday celebrating his beliefs, and he had compelled powerful men to pay lip service — that was exactly the phrase — to it.

After Farrell had written these stories for two years the desk was merciful and transferred the chore to someone else: Edwards, as it happened. Receiving this assignment was at once an infliction upon Edwards, because he was lower on the totem pole than Farrell and had to work his way up through the dirty chores; and an act of satire at his expense, and an acknowledgement that he was becoming fit to be entrusted with the tribal honor. The old men grinned with relish as they wrenched off your foreskin, but they conceded your manhood. In his new job Farrell would be obliged, since his university was fifty miles from the city, to live in the suburbs.

Mrs. Farrell thought that this would be good for the children; it was still possible, in 1944, to believe in the efficacy of the suburbs. Farrell believed, in some corner of his mind, that he would benefit by a pious atmosphere, though he was not pious. He was almost a stereotype of a newspaperman: a cynic, a drinker and occasionally a lecher (like many newspapermen he preferred liquor and talk to women), but nevertheless he felt, and he certainly was not entirely wrong, that he had been dirtied by the work he had been doing and the life he had been leading. He had been a good newspaperman, and he had liked much of the work, but he would never go back to it. Years later, when he had left the university and gone on to worldlier and better-paying jobs, if he were buying a newspaperman a drink in some bar he wouldn't take pains, as P-R men ordinarily did if they could, to make his companion aware that he knew his way around in the city room; he was no more anxious to talk about his newspaper career than a man is to mention a woman whom he is ashamed to have loved.

The night rewrite job was offered to Edwards. He had expected that Jimmy McKeon, if only for the sake of ritual and in order not to allow Edwards to feel that anybody was ready to cut fingers and become blood brothers with him, would envelop the offer in a sniffing assumption that Edwards wouldn't want to take on a job—it meant working from five in the evening until two in the morning, five nights a week—which would interfere with his patrician revels. That Edwards hadn't foreseen was a mild amusement, even (Edwards thought) an elder-brotherly concern in McKeon's manner. He realized with a jolt that the desk—why should he be surprised, when they knew so much?—knew a good deal about Margaret. Feeling outrated, he said promptly and a little coldly that he'd take the job. He gave McKeon as strong a glare as was tactful, McKeon curled the corners of his mouth in a good-natured way that meant Edwards might be sorry when he thought it over. His dark eyes glittered behind the rimless spectacles, which he kept perfectly clear, polishing them several times a day on a spotless handkerchief; those glasses and that handkerchief gave the impression of being the cleanest things in the musty, dusty room; the glasses sparkled like an obsession.

Everybody watched whenever Jimmy stood up to clean his glasses taking the handkerchief from a back pocket. His thin jittery frame leaned back now in his chair and relaxed; he seemed about to say something profoundly human or earthy, or friendly to Edwards when his phone rang; both his phones rang; he turned to them with an air of relief, as if he'd escaped a commitment. Edwards stood up, also feeling relieved—it was bad enough being in love, without being asked to expose yourself in friendship too—and went back to his desk.

His own phone rang, and he took a story from the Oakland police reporter about a supermarket robbery. "OK, kid," the police beat man said, as he always did, when he hung up; he was only about five years older than Edwards, but like all leg men he believed that the infantry is queen of battles, and that the men who merely write stories are amateurs. Being asked to write a story would seem to Ed Cassein like a reflection upon his professional status, if not actually upon his virility.

The Duration

Ed once had known how to touch-type, but this ability had withered away, partly because of the scorn of his father, who had been a beat man too. Edwards' phone rang again; simultaneously Frank Lemmon shouted indistinct instructions from the city desk.

Edwards took the call, which was from another beat man, reporting on an income tax evasion trial. As soon as he hung up Lemmon left the desk, came to Edwards' desk and unnecessarily explained what the story was about and how Edwards should handle it. Unhappy as a desk man, brooding, huge but twitchy, behind his telephones, Frank was likely to be unsettled even by so small a thing as Edwards' having had what was obviously a semi-confidential talk with McKeon, Frank's superior. Edwards could see that he was going to have to rewrite this story, probably twice, before Frank would accept it, Edwards wasn't sorry to be busy, since it meant putting off deciding whether he *had* made a mistake in accepting the night rewrite job a decision he couldn't make without doing some hard thinking, which he would just as soon have avoided about the state of his relations with Margaret.

His phone rang again; he picked it up fatalistically, convinced that it would be Margaret. If she were to call him just now he would be unable to avoid putting himself in the wrong. If he told her at once about the night rewrite job, she would think he sounded too pleased about the prospect of spending five nights a week away from her (or at least most hours of those five nights; he supposed he could go to her apartment after two; there might even be a savor to it, if for propriety's sake he left her at five, as if it were a rendezvous that could last only a couple of hours).

On the other hand, if he didn't tell her on the phone she inevitably would ask, later, "When did you find out

about this?" She was developing a wifely gift for sens-
ing reticences and imagining sinister concealments, and
a wifely talent for being at least half-right. They seemed
very married, these days. They had cooled down—they
had to; they couldn't have maintained that heat—after
their ardors when they had thought Harry was coming
home. (If their relationship had become marriage,
Harry had been relegated to the role of a mother-in-law;
accepted as a menace to their happiness to whom one of
them nevertheless was irretrievably bound, for the foreseeable future, and who therefore was better not talked
about. Edwards had toward Harry just that feeling of
helpless annoyance, inspired by relations-in-law; time
was making Edwards feel secure in possession, and he
no longer was very jealous of Harry.)

One of the things Edwards was going to have to ask
himself was: will I perhaps be a little glad to be seeing
less of Margaret, even to be making love to her less
often? He thought about this, as he reached for the
phone, and found himself swept by a mild form of the
panic that often overtakes a bachelor, well settled in a
liaison, who sees a sure thing departing from him, even
if it's by his own wish. There is no panic exactly like this
in marriage, even in the end of a marriage; the married
man feels that he can always marry again; but there
must be overtones of castration, overtones audible
enough to shake even the most self-confident amorist,
in the loss of a regular lay who has been held to a man
by his sexual abilities, but not by law.

If it had been Margaret on the phone, he might have
dropped the idea of the night rewrite job on the spot.
The desk wouldn't have thought worse of him. They
might resent his catting around, because he was young
and had an efficiency of money and a cityful of ready
girls to choose from but a difficult love affair made him

more human and vulnerable, more like them. To be in love was a responsibility, and what the desk men, harried by their wives at home and by telephones at the office, their bowels kept in an uproar as unrelentingly as Promehteus', resented in Edwards was his lack of responsibilities.

It wasn't Margaret on the phone; it was the federal beat man, with a detail he'd forgotten. Edwards sighed with relief; he drew in a deep breath of the hallucinatory gas oxygen, which induces the belief that things will turn out all right. As he'd foreseen, it took three tries before he could get the tax evasion story into a form that was acceptable to Frank. After he handed in the first version Frank read it and called Edwards up to the desk to register his points; Edwards wrote a second version. Frank read it, heaved himself up and came to Edwards' desk to make his new complaints—he had done as much shouting for Edwards' attendance upon himself as the manners of the city room allowed, and he hated exercising the authority which he was afraid to let lie unflexed. The third version got by, but as Edwards turned to leave the desk, Frank called him back and handed him a stack of rewrites, though it was late in the day—he was like a little boy who pulls a cat's tail, and then torments it in horrified fascination, hating himself and the cat.

Edwards went back to his own desk, feeling Frank watch him, and with a complete lack of emphasis put the rewrites on top of a stack already there. Twenty-five minutes later, when he handed in the first batch of four completed stories, Frank said in a worried voice, full of genuine concern: "It's almost five-thirty; you'd better give the rest of those releases back to me. I'll leave them for Cunningham."

Once he was launched on this cycle of aggression, self-loathing and remorse, from those coils he occasionally peered out at his victim and himself with a Dostoevskian flash of mordant humor, there was nothing to do but feel sorry for him and annoyed at him and hope that five-thirty would come soon, for his sake and one's own. At five-thirty, when Jack Cunningham had glided in to relieve him, priest-like with his black clothes and his confident walk and his air of being in possession of revealed truth, Frank lumbered over to the clothes tree from which he took the jacket of his shiny pinstripe suit and, in winter weather, a loud but costly-looking topcoat in a bookmaker's check — maybe he was out of Gogol, not Dostoevsky. This evening he left fifteen minutes ahead, of Edwards, who had felt constrained by expertise oblige not to give Frank back all the handouts, and in the end had to work overtime to finish up his pile.

"You're working late," Jack Cunningham observed as Edwards handed in his copy. He spoke, from habit, with a trace of sharpness and challenge; he knew that Edwards was reasonably well-fixed for money and by nature was incapable of working an unnecessary fifteen minutes for the sake of the half-an-hours overtime pay he could then claim, but he felt obliged now and then to let Edwards know that essentially he was still on probation. Another year and Edwards would be accepted into the band, and be free of this hazing.

Edwards who thought he'd suffered enough inconvenience for one day because Frank Lemmon didn't like desk work — he had made no progress at all with the problem of Margaret — answered Cunningham with a flat "Yeah," and left the office.

He swung off the cable car two blocks before his usual stop. There was a bar here where he sometimes had a couple of drinks, when he wanted to savor the evening and the happiness that lay ahead, or when, as now, he needed to think before he met Margaret. He had a happy relationship with this bar. As newspapermen went in San Francisco at that time, he wasn't a heavy drinker and (again as newspapermen went) he didn't frequent bars much — some trace of the feeling of his father and his father's contemporaries that you did your drinking in your home or your friends' homes or in your club, a feeling that had been reinforced by the odiousness of the Prohibition speakeasies, survived in him — but he could see in his fellow newspapermen the morphology of attachments between man and bar, which could grow to resemble man-woman attachments. A man could become emotionally dependent upon a bar, which provided him with company, the sense of being part of a household routine and perhaps even with sex; he could become in some measure financially dependent upon it — turning to it for liquor and meals on credit, and even small loans; he could become jealous of its attentions to others. He could flirt with other bars; bar proprietors seemed as quick as wives to learn of these flirtations, and as ready to accuse the wanderer of wasting his substance upon others when it was rightfully theirs — they might not able to claim he was wedded to their bottles, but at least he'd established a common law relationship.

It exactly suited Edwards that this bar he liked should be on a corner. No matter how elegant it is, there is something about a bar in the middle of the block that suggests a den — a place where people hide out, and are on bad terms with the world. But this corner bar was open, from several angles, to the gaze of passersby; it was a crossroads, not a refuge. In summer, when he was on his way to Margaret's from the office while it was still not time for the blackout, he could enter this bar with a flourish — with a gallop. The cable car, heavy with the authority of cast iron, ground to a near-stop in the middle of the intersection, bringing auto traffic in four directions to a halt. It was a dramatic piece of business like dropping the pilot.

Edwards swung off the car's step and in one long movement, so it felt to him, was in the bar, where the bartender, who'd seem him through the open door, already was mixing his martini. The bartender enjoyed this ritual so much that Edwards couldn't drink anything else in this bar. This bartender was a simple man, who seemed a little bruised by experience; Edwards sometimes felt as he poured the martini that he was about to say happily, something like: "I saw yuh coming, yuh can't say I didn't see yuh coming," but he never won through to utterance. Edwards used to hope he'd get the words out as you might hope to see a small animal emerge from the brush where he'd been hiding from your friendly inspection. The bartender only smiled and mentioned the weather; Edwards, still vibrating with the impetus of the cable car, would drink quickly and with gusto. "Bartender, buy that man another martini. A man who enjoys a drink that much deserves another!" a hearty mustached stranger, standing at the bar's other end, once boomed as Edwards drank down his gin.

Drinkers who appeared to have settled down in the bar for a considerable stay often spoke in a friendly way to Edwards. Plainly it made them feel better about life to brush elbows with a man they believed to be prosperous and on his way to a loving young wife and all in all so fortunate that even war couldn't touch him — why else was he in civilian clothes? Edwards knew the bartender approved of him too: he was the sort of customer bartenders like, who has a couple of drinks and goes on his way leaving a reasonable but not embarrassingly large tip, and a sense behind him that both parties have profited from the transaction instead of the feeling that on both sides—the disaster of their lives has deepened a little. All this unenvious belief in his felicity some-times made Edwards feel that he'd have to stop drink-ing here. Completely against his will he had been forced into a pretense; he had a role to maintain; at the end of the day's work, instead of being able to relax, he found himself saddled with another responsibility.

This sense of obligation tonight drove him out of the bar before he was ready to go. After two drinks he sat down—ordinarily here he drank standing, like a man who has a place to go—and ordered a third, but as the bartender put the glass down in front of him Edwards saw a flicker of disappointment and worry cross his face. Edwards drank his martini quickly and left, smiling cheerfully at the bartender, who beamed back, reassured.

Edwards thought he was not ready to face Margaret; that demanding bar, where he was interdict-ed from looking worried or even preoccupied, had made it impossible to think out exactly what he wanted to say to her. It needed thinking about. He was familiar enough with women to know that Margaret might seem to acquiesce with good grace in his taking this night assignment, might summon up and maintain for some days an air of grave congratulation at his professional advancement, might in a demonstratively undemon-strative way play patient Griselda, sitting home every evening while he was at the office—and cherish against him a resentment, because he hadn't thought her more important, most important, for which he'd have to pay. He had to consider the possibility that her resentment might take even the ultimate form of going to bed with another man.

The Duration

Edwards' emotional life customarily sailed through such known waters that he never had taken soundings to see how much water he had, or needed, under his keel; he now found himself passionately in love with Margaret, and deeply engaged with her sexually. Any level-headed perception of her to which he might briefly attain would quickly be hustled out of the room and reappear, apologetic, neatly attired as a nightmare suspicion—or as an accident of the light which had given her face that sly, secretive, complacent look. He had one of these perceptions as he left the bar—the mind, after three drinks, sometimes takes surprising and surprisingly surefooted leaps. It was the explosion of a chain of realizations, actually, starting mildly enough with one of those doubts which occasionally assail one like a lone rifle shot heard in no man's land— it probably means nothing, is the result only of over-wrought nerves, and yet it may be the warning of a disaster in the making.

The doubt that set his echoes ringing was simply the mild but gnawing reflection that, while it was possible that he was considering this nighttime work because he was a little tired of Margaret and the strain of being in love with her, equally she might be a little tired of him. The small, not unfamiliar shock of this thought set off a massive land mine—the fear that a kind of inexorable sexual logic was leading her toward sleeping with someone else.

Their sensual life, after peaking at the time when they had believed Harry was coming home, had flowed into a delta: tropical enough; steamily marshy sometimes; the current was strong; but any delta dweller may look around suddenly and think: God, it's flat. Edwards could afford to be quite realistic about the motives which had impelled Margaret to sleep with him, because it had all turned out all right; the man who has it made, in love or in finance, can risk to be, even needs to be, expansive and candid about every doubt, fear and humiliation which once yapped at his heels. Among Margaret's motives plainly had been curiosity. She'd said to Edwards, lying beside him one night not long after they'd begun making love, that she would have been sorry to have slept with only one man in her life. (There was mischief in her voice; she was inciting rape. She stretched and waited for what she was sure would happen.) She had come to her second man with a deeper excitement than when she'd climbed, a virgin, into her bridal bed; she knew now what sex was and was randily ready to find out what else it could be; she was poised and primed to proclaim: Vive la difference!

Edwards had been first delighted, then aroused and finally a little dismayed at her readiness for sexual experimentation.

"What do you want me to do?" she murmured, and kept on murmuring. He had just about outrun his experience and his inventiveness.

She even shocked him a little; she seemed to him to be taking the wrong tack; while he felt, increasingly, that she was his wife, she appeared to feel, increasingly, that she was his mistress. The entrepreneur who creates a market also calls into existence the possibility of competitors. Of course, Harry existed; Margaret's roused imagination must some injuries try the experiment of juxtaposing herself and Harry in the moves she had newly learned. Edwards' only ultimate achievement might be to make Harry's bed livelier. Edwards was prepared to accept that possibility; what unsettled him was the realization that the appetite for experimentation he had quickened to life in Margaret might in due course lead her to experimentation with another lover.

[115]

He was worse off than Pygmalion, who may sometimes have regretted he hadn't left Galatea marble, but didn't have to worry about his girl's speculating whether another man's chisel could do more for her.

In fact, Margaret threatened to become the girl her manner always had implied she was. She was not unaware of this.

"You've loosed a monster on the world," she murmured, kneeling naked before Edwards and resting her head against his knees as she embraced them. Her tone, like her attitude, spoke only of respect and contentedness; but even if she didn't intend to state a demand upon him, it was necessarily present in her words. Edwards never before had deeply cared whether he kept or lost a girl so he never had grasped the remorseless logic of lust: that sex leads to more sex, as murder leads to more murder. Having helped himself to another man's wife, he now glimpsed the ironic possibility that he might become like the murderer who is genuinely shocked by the immorality of capital punishment. He saw too that, if the black day came when Margaret plainly intended to wander further afield, it would be no more use asking her for mercy than it would have been for Macbeth to plead with Macduff; Macbeth had said to Macduff the only possible thing.

Nevertheless, he would have liked to say to her: Dear Margaret, can't we go back to innocence? (By which of course he meant a relative state: not too innocent to sleep with him, but innocent enough not to try another man, innocent enough not to make impossible demands upon his sexual athleticism.) But Margaret, dancing lewdly and happily on the shores of the lagoon to which he'd voyaged her, obviously had no regrets at having left the temperate zones forever.

He stood on the sidewalk, just outside the bar and

out of sight of those deluded drinkers who imagined his life was so crammed with felicity, as all this passed through his mind. A cable car ground by; its relentless iron passage beat upon his nerves like an affirmation of the universe's massive indifference to pain; its noise might have been the clamor of a train bearing down on him, as he lay strapped to the tracks, and if he had been such a victim he couldn't have felt more convinced of the reality of horror. The car passed; some sort of normality flooded back; but in those instants his view of Margaret had altered forever. A hostility to her had been borne or been helped to birth. He had imagined her promiscuity so vividly, it had become a fact of a sort, as the behavior to us, in dreams, of other people is real in a way: we hold them accountable, wary with the ancient suspicion that we know more when asleep than awake.

The wish to have another drink, frustrated by the sight of the bartender's impending disillusion, still throbbed within him like an unanswered telephone call. His will was weak and his temper peevish, after the crisis through which he'd just passed; the three drinks he'd had surged through him like medicine, which had been administered to him by a kindly doctor who now was advising him that, though there seemed little chance he had contracted the deadly ailment he had feared, the possibility remained: while it remained, he should pamper and indulge himself, refuse the world's demands upon him. It was bitterly true; he couldn't be *sure* that Margaret wouldn't be unfaithful to him or even sure that she hadn't already been unfaithful to him — unfaithful was the way he put it, and he believed, without any satisfaction that she would see it that way too. The imperfect nature of certainty was not Margaret's fault nevertheless, he felt she had committed the fault of Caesar's wife, and he went off to find another bar, where he sat and thought and drank until he was inflamed with possessiveness; he would go to her apartment and lay her, so grandly and lasciviously that it wouldn't matter whether she was a good girl or a bitch: in either case her essential nature would be working in his behalf. The practical thought followed that this course would cut short reproaches and demands to know where he'd been and why he was so stiff.

He went out into the chilly dark, slightly misty street. Reality, like drops of foggy moisture, began to coalesce and attach itself to him. He no longer believed that Margaret was likely to be unfaithful to him. He no longer believed, either, that it would be easy to go to bed with her the minute he walked into her apartment, or that he would escape explanations.

He had some trouble with the lock on Margaret's apartment door; when at last he got the key to work, he threw the door open imperiously, nearly hitting Margaret, who was on her way to open it.

She threw her arms around him. "Oh!" she said. "I thought you weren't coming." He noticed she seemed slightly tight.

He looked over her shoulder and saw, on the table in her little kitchen, an open bottle of champagne and one glass. She withdrew from his arms and explained, "I got a raise. I thought you weren't coming, when you didn't call I started to worry and then I got angry—I don't know why I decided nothing had happened to you; it isn't like you to stop off at a bar, but I decided that's what you'd done; where were you, anyway?—anyway, I decided to celebrate by myself."

It was something to celebrate. Wages, as well as prices, were frozen by government decree; in practice,

employers could safely ignore this restriction (the government made no attempt to enforce it, rightly considering that it could rely on the employers to do so) but
naturally it didn't often happen that an employer chose
to do so—especially in the case of a secretarial job, in a
city overstocked with girls.

Edwards explained that he had been discussing
with Jimmy McKeon—which was true, in a way—the
possibility of taking the job of night rewrite man. He
added—which was perfectly true, for he had seen the
right thing to do as he walked through the sobering
mist that he had decided against taking it, both because
of Margaret and for reasons of realpolitik. It was better,
for the sake of advancement, to stay close to the sources
of power; if he did a good job on night rewrite, he'd be
in danger of lodging in that backwater of a job.

Margaret glowed at him, and said she admired his
shrewdness; which was true, in more senses than at the
moment she thought she meant, for in the long run how
could she have thought him anything but dumb to have
curtailed his nights with her? He went out to buy more
champagne from the liquor store owner who looked
like John Silver. He asked for cigarettes, hoping that his
festive purchase might win him a pack of Camels or
Luckies but the pirate merely gave him a look like
Henry Morgan quelling somebody who'd questioned
his division of the loot, and slammed down on the
counter two packs of an almost unsmokable brand.

They spent a maudlin and loving evening, and
woke next morning feeling faintly ashamed, but bound
to one another. Sentimentality, to minds, which distrust
it, can link a man and woman more firmly, with more of
a feeling of a commitment which has gone too far to be
revoked, than any other shared erotic practice. Leaving
the building around ten, he ran smack into Mrs. Arnold,

the landlady. To his amazement, she nodded to him pleasantly and even with a little deference—rather like the proprietor of a good restaurant greeting a valued patron he hasn't seen for some time.

It seemed the omen of a day in which things couldn't go wrong for him. His interview with McKeon went off well. The city editor accepted his altered decision without surprise, even with a certain relief - as if, Edwards thought, McKeon felt he had done himself an injury by asking Edwards to do something so much out of character (that is, as McKeon pictured Edwards' character; McKeon thought him more frivolous than he was) as to work nights. McKeon must feel almost as if he had offered Edwards a bribe to ask someone to exhibit more determination of purpose than you believe he possesses is a form of bribery, like training a dog by holding a goodie just above his normal reach. Edwards had refused the bribe, and McKeon, though regretting the lost profit both might have had, was somberly glad to have both their integrities saved.

Euphoric, he went to Margaret at the day's end and found her sitting, stricken and drawn-faced among disaster. She handed him a letter from her mother.

Her mother's handwriting was intimidating—large, firm, its regularity of form conceding nothing to intimacy. Just to get a letter from Margaret's mother—she was an addict of the telephone—was intimidating; it was like receiving a proclamation. The tone of this letter was formal as a proclamation's. She wrote that she had heard a story about Margaret which she hoped and believed was not true. She understood that Margaret had begun her marriage under difficult conditions, but—this was the part of the letter in which she struck her native Vermont note most forcibly—conditions were nearly always difficult, and marriage was seldom easy. Differences in upbringing, native region, and religious faith had divided her from Margaret's father (why, Margaret thought rebelliously at this point, must parents always leap from embarrassing you by discussing your life to embarrassing you by discussing theirs?)—but they had made a commitment and, she believed, neither of them ever had wavered in it. She hoped to hear from Margaret soon.

It was perfectly done. It left Margaret no recourse. She couldn't accuse her mother of accepting scandal too easily; it was plain to her that her mother was in full possession of the facts. If her mother hadn't been sure of her ground, she would have telephoned, and beaten around the bush. (How she had found out, Margaret couldn't imagine; but there were a hundred possible avenues of disclosure, in this compact city where everybody lived jammed up against everybody else; she and John had been lucky to get away with it as long as they had.)

If her mother had ranted and railed at her, Margaret who was fond of her mother but hadn't always found her sympathetic - could have invoked old resentments; she could have summoned up her old partisanship, for her father against her mother, she could have felt, had no more right to be angry at Edwards, whom she didn't know, than, years ago she had had a right to be angry at her husband, whom (her daughter had felt) she didn't know. She even could have found emotional, if not rational, support in her Catholicism, toward which her mother's attitude always had been coolly skeptical and deprecating—odd as it might seem to invoke her (former) religion in behalf of adultery, the emotions, when warfare breaks out, are not too particular about where they look for allies.

The letter might not have hit Margaret so hard if she

and Edwards hadn't just had a bad pregnancy scare, which finally proved baseless. Harry and Margaret had decided before he went overseas that they wouldn't have children until he came back; but they had been careless a few times, and it troubled Margaret that nothing had come of it. She believed herself to be a healthy creature meant to bear, and to bear easily; she had the look of a woman like that. She wasn't sure how really careless, on her side, those carelessnesses had been. When Harry left she was certain she was pregnant, though she had no reason for thinking so. Sailors were supposed to knock up girls and then sail away, leaving them singing the blues or arias; Margaret had a rollicking sense of having knocked up Harry. She wrote, in her head, the letter which would break the news to him — it was a magnificent letter; not being able to send it infuriated her so much that her affection for Harry dried up a little as if she had sent the letter and he hadn't answered. But when Harry was barely gone she looked so smug her woman friends thought she must be glad to be rid of him, or must have a boy friend, or must be carrying a child: they also speculated on interesting combinations of these possibilities.

To find that this certainty that she that had conceived was based on total error had unnerved Margaret; she felt a profound doubt of her own capabilities. Sometimes, if they had been drinking, she took risks with Edwards; next day, mildly ill with apprehension, she would wonder if she were driven by a necessity to prove to herself that she was fruitful. Last month, when she had good reason to think she was pregnant, she had experienced all the sensations of a gambler who has successfully courted a disaster he is half in love with. Naturally her most rending worry had been what her parents would think of her (Harry had been still partly a stranger to her when they had parted, and had become now almost entirely one); in her Mother's case Margaret's consideration had been focused not only on what would her mother think, but what would her mother say? She could count on her father to be gentle.

This crisis had passed; but to receive this letter now gave her a sensation that her mother must have known of her terrible predicament: her mother was in league with righteousness, with which she shared a gaze from which you could not hide. Margaret believed in righteousness, though she no longer believed that righteousness has eyes; still, she couldn't help feeling at times that *someone* was watching her; probably, she told herself practically, this was because of the many times she had jumped out of her bed, where Edwards was, and gone naked to the telephone to hear her mother's voice. (After five minutes Margaret would say: "Hold on a minute, mother, will you? I just got out of the shower. It's *cold* up here, you know." She had invoked this formula so many times it was no wonder her mother was convinced of her guilt; she must think Margaret was trying to wash it away.)

Explanations for what she could only call a sense of sinfulness were really no help, though: sometimes quite the reverse. Margaret had been apprised, by reading Freud, of the true nature of her love for her father and her occasional hostility toward her mother; Freud had done her the disservice of piling conscious guilt on unconscious guilt; crushed beneath the weight of what every irrational instinct assured her were twenty-two years of wrongdoing and disloyalty, Margaret cowered before her mother's letter.

Edwards, who was drained by his own emotional storm the day before and slightly hung over besides, was unable to rise to the occasion. He could only hold her. They clung together, in that bleak little apartment, as if waiting for a knock on the door.

The next night and the third night, he merely held her in his arms. The fourth night they made love. The fifth night they made love. The sixth night Margaret was sullen; her eyes, when he arrived at her apartment, were red. The seventh night they made love. On the eighth day, a letter arrived for him, special delivery, at the newspaper. She wrote that it was ended. Her letter, which she clearly meant to be a letter that he could keep as a memorial of her, was typewritten on two sheets of cheap yellow paper, on both sides of the paper. It was touching, and invoked her presence for him—he could see her ripping a sheet out of her battered portable (a worn and collegiate thing, like an old pair of saddle shoes), and turning the paper over, too absorbed in her emotion even to reach for another sheet—but even in that moment of great distress he felt, a little annoyed, that she could have taken a little more care with the letter's form. A postscript said she was making up a package, which she would mail to his apartment, containing the change of shirts and the razor and toothbrush he kept in her apartment. A second postscript spoke of complete despair. He went to see her that evening. She was unsurprised to see him, and, calm and firm in her resolve.

Next morning was fine and sunny, as mornings after disaster are: it rained, the morning of Waterloo, but next day Napoleon must have waked to sunlight, or its equivalent, human cheerfulness which, however kindly meant, would have had its ultimate root in the relief of those around him that they weren't emperors.

Jimmy McKeon, that morning, glanced a couple of times at Edwards and thanked god he wasn't loved and wasn't in love. Still, on the night before, as the door of

The Duration

Margaret's apartment closed behind Edwards, what he
felt certainly contained a very large measure of relief.
Napoleon tried suicide, but earlier; not after Waterloo.
Finality is blessedly soothing.

[NINE]

Edwards had a special reason for relief. Another girl was on the horizon. He had been feeling a little regret at having to pass up the opportunity she seemed to present; once or twice he even had given his love for Margaret a thorough inspection, to determine if like Nelson it had a convenient blind eye; no use; he had signed Margaret's articles, in blood. But now he could crowd on sail, raise the Jolly Roger. She seemed to him an especially valuable prize because she appeared to promise far less involvement than Margaret. It was no season for commitment. That spring was a time of widespread emotional exhaustion, frustration and peevishness. It was clear that the war was won.

The Allies mudded their way up Italy, the Americans boated and bazooka'd across the Pacific; the Russians, marching maybe over the bones of Teutonic Knights and Polish kings who had dreamed of reigning in the Kremlin, once again pursued retreating invaders through the Ukraine, the Baltic states, Poland;

The Duration

Germany's cities cringed under furious skies. The invasion of Western Europe couldn't be far off. Death-spattered as this going-ashore promised to be, with behind it looming a worse bloodletting if Japan had to be invaded, the national mood was for getting it over with. People had been stretched on the rack for too long. Many couples were tired out by involvements like Edwards and Margaret's; many wives had been worn down, to the point of losing most of their capacity for deep anxiety, by worry about their husbands.

The deprivations of rationing and consumer good shortages were enervating, like the deprivations of poverty; it was no disgrace to be at war, but it might as well be. Berserker impulses, a wish to assault the enemy headlong, to "slay and make bound all that shall resist" were mounting among civilians too; Hitler's wasn't the only head that in early 1944 was ringing with *Gotterdammerung*. America was one great dull throb of: have at them!

This sullen, heavy and charged atmosphere bore down upon Edwards, and added to his private fatigues. His sturdy good nature was chipping and weathering and flawing. The minor daily strains involved in being a civilian, the major strain of his predicament with Margaret, and the two tensions' theme in common - that he was Margaret's civilian lover - were shepherding him toward irrationality. He felt an increasing disposition to dislike any man in uniform; he very nearly swung on a Marine Corps lieutenant who stepped on his foot in an elevator and didn't apologize.

Even against his dear boon-bane, Margaret, a bill of particulars he'd been accumulating; but before he'd reached the point of thinking hazy thoughts of a declaration of independence—a declaration which certainly never would have been made—she'd handed him his freedom. Even before this emancipation, even before Lee Highsmith had appeared, he had been listening to internal orators who assured him that it would serve Margaret right if he had an affair with another girl: he owed it to his nerves to sooth them. Oddly enough, now that he was free he still needed this justification. Once the initial shock of dismissal had worn off, he found he didn't really believe in this parting from Margaret, he still felt bound to her; foolish and hopeful as a Jacobite king, though expelled by his kingdom he believed himself under an obligation to it and seldom doubted his restoration.

Yet this moral unease had the effect too of propelling him toward his new girl; after his season with Margaret, conscious guilt had become an essential ingredient of sex for him. It was another injury that Margaret had done him; once he started finding occasion to blame Margaret, it was as easy as finding fault with militarism.

He had militarism to thank, though, for Lee. As the manpower demands of the armed forces grew, the city's newspapers were obliged to fill out their staffs with girls just out of college: journalism majors, even English majors. Lee was one of these. She was a girl from Wyoming, said to be the daughter of a very rich rancher; she'd gone to the University of California at Berkeley. She worked for the *Binnacle,* which was a little less hard-shelled about hiring such girls than the *Observer.*

Edwards ran into her occasionally on the sort of small story that her desk would send her out on, and that a reporter like Edwards might find himself assigned to if there wasn't anyone else handy: an interview with a visiting author, a talk with the wife of a minor war hero, a Commonwealth Club luncheon if the speaker was considered second-echelon (Walter Lippmann on the program, for instance, rated Lee; any brigadier general would have been accorded all-male coverage by the city desks of the four dailies).

On a spring Sunday morning in 1944 Edwards, hung over, was dispatched to cover the Red Mass in St. Mary's Cathedral, an annual rite attended by Roman Catholic lawyers. Archbishop Mitty was to deliver the sermon. In front of the cathedral, a child's mud pile executed in red brick, Edwards encountered Lee, striding along in her rocking cowgirl's gait. She was a cougar-colored girl: pale tawny eyes, ash-blonde hair, skin so white it suggested always having been sheltered under a ten-gallon hat. She was wearing a beige gabardine suit; under her arm she carried a large bag of neutral-colored leather, which might have contained emergency rations of jerky and water, or of Strasbourg pate and Remy Martin. Her style and ambience were confusing, or novel—Neiman-Marcus hadn't yet crossbred Dallas and Paris—or maybe hadn't melded yet. Her shoes matched her bag; above them her nice white legs were un-nyloned. Her white gloves and expensive-looking spring straw hat seemed mere bits of schoolgirl elegance; a sort of statement she would be able to discard when she'd done a little more work on her identity.

Her voice had a grate or a creak in it: a harshness that was clearly an inland sound, the rasp of a corral gate maybe, not the erotic groan of a boat against a dock. This is not to say that her voice was not erotic. Like a whiskey throat, it suggested a blunt, direct approach to pleasure.

Edwards didn't want to sit through mass or to hear encomiums for the legal profession, or to hear Archbishop Mitty, a pedestrian orator; he did want to get a drink for his hangover (there was a good bar across the street in the Richelieu Hotel) and to improve his acquaintance with this moon maid or Rosalind — disguised-as-a-young-man or Annie Oakley or whatever she was, so he proposed: "Let's go have a drink. You don't need to cover this, I can tell you exactly what the archbishop'll say. I'll make up some quotes for you."

She hesitated, but she said: "I'd like to, but I don't think I should."

They stood looking into one another's eyes; she appeared to be waiting for him to advance some more persuasive argument, but he was too debilitated for ingenuity. He said: "Well" — taking her by the elbow, so that she wouldn't suppose he wanted a drink more than he wanted her, although at the moment this was very near the truth — "I'll tell you, I'll have my drink, and you listen to the archbishop, and I'll bet you that tomorrow afternoon the *Call* and the *News* will pick up more quotes from my story than they will from yours."

The *Call-Bulletin* and the *News* were the afternoon papers, not much given to covering Sunday happenings, which mostly they rewrote from the morning papers. She smiled broadly. This evidently was the right approach: the road to this Desdemona's bed lay through the occupational pitch: how much easier it'd have been for Othello (not all those afternoons of talk) if Desdemona had been a WAC second lieutenant, in love with the self-assured toughness of the military profession.

"All right," she said. She gave Edwards a kind of half-salute, half-wave of adieu with one of the white-gloved hands, and started up the cathedral's steps. Edwards watched the trim behind and pretty bare legs for a minute and then hurried across Van Ness Avenue to the bar, where he had three drinks, decided it was time to be checking in with the desk, had a fourth drink

and did telephone the desk. Frank Lemmon was conso-
latory and mocking over the necessity of Edwards' having to drag himself out on such a chore on a Sunday
morning; he sounded unharried by anything so
Edwards decided that instead of going back to the office
on the streetcar he could afford to take the time to walk
back, down Geary Street, sobering as he went. On the
way he stopped for a fifth drink.

In the office Lemmon was invisible behind the
Sunday paper. A single reporter was working on a pile
of rewrites, tapping out a few words, glancing at the
release he was working from, then typing a few more
words, all with an expression of distaste which hardly
could have been exceeded if he had been occupied in
doing public relations for Buchenwald. A lone photographer, moved by the Sunday necessity of taking something apart and improving it, had dismantled his camera; a lone copygirl sat on the copyboys' bench, picking
at her nail polish; the assistant news editor and the wire
editor were telling one another stories; two men at the
copy desk scribbled silently. Relatively speaking, the
room was so empty and so quiet that those who were
there seemed half-apologetic, as if they were guests at a
not very fashionable party to which few people had
come. Edwards wrote his story and turned it in to
Lemmon who grunted O.K. behind his paper when
Edwards said he was going to lunch. Edwards ate a
large lunch and was sober when he went back to the
city room.

Monday afternoon the *Call* and the *News* used only
Edwards' invented quotes; none of Lee's real ones.
Tuesday morning she telephoned and said she wanted
to congratulate him.

"How did you know so well, the sort of thing he'd
say?" she asked. "You aren't a Catholic, are you?"

"No, I'm not."

"I didn't think you were. I asked somebody who said you weren't." It was quite clearly a declaration of interest.

Edwards enjoyed it for a moment - there is no pleasure in sex exactly like this first commitment — then asked her to have a drink with him at six. She said she would.

As soon as he was launched upon this new endeavor he began to have doubts about its wisdom. It was clear that he could not make a side dish of her or even have much of anything else on the menu. Plainly she had expectations of him. At first he thought it was just a case of her being a girl from the hinterland fascinated with San Francisco, and delighted with him because he was an indigene. He mentioned a dinky and she looked puzzled; the pale eyes glowed with pleasure and interest when he explained it was the native word for a cable car (purists said, for one kind of cable car). Since her fancy was for local color, he obliged her: he drove past, and pointed out to her, his grandfather's former town house, which had been only two blocks and one hour away from being dynamited when the Fire at last was brought under control.

He sensed her, in the dark, radiating amusement and enjoyment as they climbed the unlighted wooden staircase to Izzy Gomez' bar. She relished the dumbwaiter in which the meals came down from the kitchen at the Manger; she smiled ruefully at nearly blind old Fred Solari at his restaurant's cash register, unwilling to trust anyone else to handle his money. Edwards scrounged up some black market gas coupons and they made the trip to Los Altos, where at L'Omelette there was the radio behind the bar on which Pierre found and played (for himself) Bach and Hindemith, indifferent to the musical tastes of his patrons.

The Duration

Edwards showed her how to get a drink if you were out on the town after midnight. (The bars closed at twelve, two hours earlier than in peacetime. Report said this deprivation was to be blamed upon the teetotaling wife of an important general; its effect was that between eleven and twelve the convinced drinkers consumed at breakneck speed, and at midnight staggered into the streets in exactly the state which the general's lady had intended to proscribe to them.) You went to the Mark or the Fairmont and took an elevator to any floor, then walked along the corridor until you came to a door with the sounds of a party behind it. You rang, and chances were the door was opened by a flushed and whooping stranger in uniform who dragged you inside and pressed drinks on you. Edwards thought the welcome was warmer for a civilian than it would have been for another man in uniform, against whose insignia the men behind the door might have held specific grudges or maintained a rivalry; there may have been a kind of chivalry in those generous greetings, a pity for the man who, for whatever reason, was so out of things; and of course another girl always was welcome.

Weeks went by and Lee's gaze continued to glow at him; her gloved hand rested lightly on his sleeve as they sat at bars in San Francisco, Marin, Alameda, and San Mateo counties and he told her San Francisco's newspaper legends; companionably, at the end of an evening, she invited him into her apartment for a drink, and companionably she threw him out, without any sense of an ultimate decision. Her apartment was luxurious by comparison with Margaret's; it was on Telegraph Hill, looking down on the Embarcadero, and smartly furnished. He approved of Lee's having money; Edwards didn't believe that the rich are different from you and me: he believed, with some reason that the rich were like him, even if his parents were some distance from being wealthy. The Goebbels-like segment of his mind which was busy with the task of downgrading Margaret advanced the theory that if Margaret had been a little better bred she never would have put up with that apartment of hers! She would have found a better apartment (Dr. Goebbels didn't explain how).

In Margaret's shabby apartment he had only been able to enjoy love and great bodily pleasure, and they had been either not enough for him or too much for him; so he found it soothing now to sit at Lee's big window, drinking her good bourbon, and watch the midnight lights and the scurrying and general air of sailing with the dawn tide that prevailed on the pier, at the hill's foot, where an escort aircraft carrier was tied up. Of course Lee's manners and her manner weren't superior to Margaret's; quite the reverse; but the ease with which she lived with her money was a kind of good manners that made up for her other deficiencies. Besides, to him she was exotic. He liked the sensation that if he looked into her bedroom closet he'd find something silken from Paris hanging alongside a pair of cowboy's chaps. He liked her earthiness: he took her to a bar where a huge Negro played the bass and emphatically boomed out the blunt lyrics of "I Used to Work in Chicago"; Lee listened with smiling attention, seeming to relish a memory about which she might or might not tell Edwards one of these days, and remarked that one of the verses they'd just heard was new to her.

Sitting in Lee's obviously costly apartment, in which he already had marked out the articles of furniture and the rugs on which he hoped to have Lee, and the manners in which he hoped to have her — in the midst of these imagined improprieties Edwards had that sense of regained propriety, of having returned to

one's proper framework, which is immensely comforting to someone who has been unlucky in love — they
embrace, but they do not know the secret in the million-
aire's heart. Also comforting is the prospect that one's
letch is soon to be gratified, but not so easily as to seem
cheap in comparison with what's been lost. In fact he
was terribly pleased with Lee until it dawned on him
what the light in her eyes was all about: then he
recoiled. He felt as if, having just staggered ashore from
the wreck of the *Vestris*, he'd proposed to console himself by spending some time in an amusement park with
a girl, and been told by her: no, she didn't fancy two
tickets for the tunnel of love — what she wanted was to
take a trip on that excursion boat, the *General Slocum* she
thought its name was.

Unhappy love wasn't in Edwards' style; he felt this,
and he minded the damage to his view of himself almost
as much as he disliked the pain of his unhappiness over
Margaret. He had a physical sense of himself as a small,
self-possessed, self-sufficient man. His Orkney tweed
topcoat completed this sensation of being a neat package; wearing it on a brisk, chill, gray day he would go
down the city's hills in long steps, jaunty as a jockey, as
a small general of Marines, as a Russian politician wearing a fur cap at an airport to greet the frozen envoys of
the west. He was not known as a vain man, but his
drinking friends sometimes noticed with resentment the
quick small look of satisfaction he shot from the corner
of his eye at his own tweeded figure in the mirror
behind the bar, as he patted them on the shoulder and
abandoned them on the stools which he could leave but
to which they must cling.

Still, it can be dangerous not to cling to anything.
Edwards' barroom companions hadn't yet seen the
application of this truth to him, but they would, and in

another four years there would be veiled but malicious speculation, after he left the bar, on why he'd never married. This speculation of course would miss the point: his choice in sterilities would have been to esteem himself, not to love other men. Yet, that could come too; much as Edwards liked girls, a sense in a moral man that he isn't leading a normal life—which for Edwards ultimately would mean a family life—can unnerve him into true divagations. Perhaps Margaret, jolting him off course, really had put him back in his proper orbit; in weakening and lessening him, had restored to him the strength—which he rapidly had been losing—to make and endure a marriage.

The shock had been severe. It was to his credit that he felt as little as humanly could be expected of hurt vanity, of angry humiliation that Margaret had dismissed him. What bothered Edwards were the indignities he had done to himself. He'd committed all the classic follies: loitering around her apartment house late at night to see if she came home with other men, running after girls in the street he thought looked like her, exacerbating his nerves by starting to telephone her and then hanging up.

He pictured her at the moment when she spread her legs to receive the phallus, flushed and peremptory, of another man. (It was a symptom of his disease that he'd ceased to credit her with any hesitations at all; he firmly believed she was already in bed with someone else.) To sleep with other girls relieved but didn't assuage him; they were less use to him than he was to them. "Who is she?" they said, sadly or amusedly. "If you see her again," one girl said, "Tell her I'll buy her a bottle of scotch, after the war. She is a scotch drinker, isn't she?" asked this sturdy girl from Indiana, a hearty consumer of bourbon and branch water.

The Duration

He must put his hopes on Lee, who gave intimations that she also was recovering from a disaster. Slowly, cautiously but compulsively she began to draw for Edwards the portrait of her lost or truant love. It was like watching an artist wander by a drawing board beneath which lies a piece of charcoal. He picks up the charcoal and idly draws a line, and moves on. A little later he strolls by the board again and draws another line, apparently unrelated, to the first. Next time he goes by, it appears to strike him that something can be done with those lines; he makes a little design, he stands back and looks at it, and then all pretense is dropped and he goes to work in earnest, ignoring everybody around him.

Lee's first line was a casual reference to a guy I used to "a guy I used to go out with..." She told a story about how he'd ridden a horse into a Laramie restaurant on a bet. A couple of days later he reappeared in her talk, this time as ". . . someone" ". . . someone once took me dancing at this place in Denver..." This time Edwards heard the strained note in her voice. Two days later it was: "This guy I used to date . . ." Then suddenly she burst out with "Bob used to tell me . . ." apparently having revolved Edwards and her old lover in her mind so much that she'd forgotten Edwards didn't know Bob's name, and officially at least wasn't even supposed to know Bob's importance, though for some days past when she mentioned "someone" or "this guy" it had been with a certain coquetry, as if it were implicit between them that Edwards had a rival whom, out of tact she was not mentioning directly.

Quite apart from the fact that nobody who is sick wants to be told about somebody else's disease, it made Edwards impatient to think he would have to hear all about Bob. He knew more or less what Bob would be like. He was good-looking and charming; he drank too much; his parents had spoiled him and still did; he was irresponsible. He borrowed money from Lee and didn't pay it back (she might or might not admit that she believed he spent it on other girls). He would be either a flier or a private in the medical corps. He was sexually inconsiderate. On a summer afternoon in the country he made her get into the back seat of his small, cramped English Ford, and made love to her even though he had no precautions handy; afterwards when she believed she was pregnant, he showed no concern. He made love to her in a closet, during a party when they might have been found at any minute. It would never occur to her that she didn't have to get into the Ford's back seat, or could have left the closet. He would have some sort of male trappings that had impressed Lee; a $300 wrist watch, or shoes made in England, or a solid gold razor.

Edwards would have to suffer under the implication that he could be improved by wearing a $300 wrist watch, or shoes made in England, or using a solid gold razor. But all this gave Edwards pause, too, because she had suffered hurt and he didn't want to injure her further. He hesitated; he relaxed his pressure upon her; she felt this, and not just because of such obvious circumstances as that he didn't call her so often and was less urgent with her when they wound up an evening at her apartment, drinking and making restricted love. But this slacking of pace, this caution had exactly the opposite effect from what he intended. Across restaurant tables, while he ate chicken Raphael Weill and she ate steak (waiters seemed to recognize that she had a rancher's deep need for steaks and, in this year when steak had been ostentatiously crossed off most menus, would volunteer the belief that one could be found for the lady), the catamount eyes thanked him for what she took to be his courtesy.

The message he got was that he had only to wait for her to ripen. How could he dislike this? His reservations melted in her new warmth: always before he had thought of her as very female but not very womanly. Even her clothes had become softer and gentler; much less leather was in evidence. If she had asked him to ride with her one Sunday in the Park and had appeared mounted sidesaddle he wouldn't have been surprised.

Edwards hadn't taken into account the cumulative effects of shared time. It took these moments of sudden, unexpected communication across a restaurant table to make him realize what a steady day-in-and-day-out intimacy they'd achieved. Without having been to bed, they had a considerable knowledge of each other's bodies; each knew his way around in the furniture of the other's life. The substantial sum of what they knew about each other, when contrasted with the vital things they didn't know about each other, gave them a delicious feeling of playing at sex as children play at being married.

They were becoming as fascinated with one another as bad children in a corner. But they weren't bad children, they were good children, which certainly entitled them to be bad children later. He saw that she was absorbed in studying his restraint, and in considering the force that must be building up behind it, she was observing her own restraint, and wondering what would happen when it broke. Sometimes, in the course of those long vinous dinners in which they sat with their knees jammed together under the table, he would gleam alcoholically and lustfully at her, not saying anything; and her eyes would light from his gleam, and gleam back at him. But when finally she went to bed with him it was with a sad humorousness—as if she were saying she wasn't to be outdone in courtesy, would have felt herself deficient in good manners to keep him waiting any longer; sad because she was acknowledging that, for him at least, love appeared out of the question. A happy time began for Edwards. He and Lee did not expect too much from each other or hope for too much from each other: their relationship had the ease of an old friendship. More precisely, it had the ease of comrades who have been through a good deal of danger. Sex could not shoot them down from ambush, when they rode so easily, weapons at the ready, eyes scanning the brush.

Edwards sometimes had seen the same assurance in the relationship of powerful but shady men—underworld lords, gambling casino proprietors, nightclub owners—with their pretty mistresses. Mated for the season, they loped with the grace, confidence and slightly showy contempt of the great felines through the buffalo herds baffled by the dust that domesticity raises. To have extracted from love and from marriage their flavor and nutrition, and distilled out their side effects—that was achievement. Later, in retrospect, when he thought of their time together the image that rose was of Lee's slender white bare arm lying supple and relaxed beside his sleeve on some bar. While they talked and laughed, their arms were aware of each other as dogs, lying at their owner's feet, are aware of their owner's and of each other.

Around ten-thirty or so he might tap her arm. "Let's go." If she wanted to stay for another drink it was only his flesh that was incommoded, not his soul that was bruised. He had no wish ever to be in love again. They were as lighthearted as strangers who have met, somewhere on a weekend, and fallen into each other's arms;

after the weekend, perhaps it will go on, perhaps not. For the moment they had no questions to put, no demands to make except those that would evoke only pleased complaisance. Their love or whatever it was called — they didn't call it anything — stayed lively because nothing about it was agreed: it remained rife with possibility. They preserved a ceremonial distance.

At first, Edwards would telephone her each afternoon, or sometimes after he had gone home from work, and ask if he would be seeing her that evening. This etiquette eroded, and soon they simply met each evening in a bar. (He never went directly to her apartment, as he had to Margaret's.) Formal recognition of their autonomy remained; one or the other always would ask gravely, in a voice that disclaimed possessiveness, as they parted in the morning; "See you at quarter of six?" He spent nearly every night in her apartment. Leaving in the morning was less difficult than in the building where Margaret lived. There were only six apartments in Lee's building, all at high rentals so there were not any people to dodge and they seemed worldly. Some gave Edwards such worldly looks, he became afraid they thought he was sponging off Lee, and occasionally he'd insist she spend the night in his apartment. She complained that he didn't dust enough. As a woman she was neither very tidy nor very untidy, but she had a plainswoman's distrust of the insinuative powers of dust.

Suddenly she stopped complaining. He saw she had realized that each complaint was driving them closer to facing up to the question of whether it wasn't silly of them — self-indulgent, even considering how desperate the need in the city for living quarters was to continue living apart. Separately they pondered and separately they decided for separateness and noncommitment. Lee brought the matter into daylight—she was the woman and it was her role to seem practical. As if following a ritual which each was relieved to discover the other knew, they numbered and noted the arguments for and against living together, and agreed they were better off each keeping his own quarters—their tone was so sensible, you would have thought they were discussing a hygenic but slightly embarrassing precaution. "Anyway, there wouldn't be room for your books in my place," Lee said, laughing nervously, as if even to have admitted the perils of commitment was more commitment than she cared for.

He continued to make love to her as eagerly and with as delicious a triumph as if he had bedded another man's wife; but it was the unknown man who finally would claim her, that he was forestalling; it was time itself he was robbing. Their affair had the refreshing quality of being on an atoll—never knowing when the ship would call that would end their adventure, and not feeling obliged to care. The toast she served him each morning was made from breadfruit. Their bed seemed like a beach—he was forever surprised she stayed so white. Even on a real beach, she neither reddened nor tanned. She was a wonder: a whiteness to add to Melville's catalog of whiteness. She was all simplicities; he had thought beforehand, of love with her as a straight line, a long straight thrust, and he found what he had expected.

In time Edwards began to think about marriage. The idea crept up on him comfortably—like the conviction after playing a few hands that luck be with you tonight, or the feeling while you lie pleasantly drowsing after waking that today the weather will be fine. Both beliefs require testing—you have to be dealt more cards; you have to look out the window, and look out again an hour later. In the instance of women, Edwards thought pleasantly, you have to keep on laying them for a while. He knew of course that it wasn't within miles of being so simple as that, but it was part of Lee's growing hold on him that she was so entirely and flatteringly at his disposal. Do unto me, she said. It sounded golden after the rigors imposed on him by Margaret's unspoken demand: Do unto me better than others can do. Lee's lack of pressure upon him was pleasing also to his sense of pace. He was an unhurried man, by temperament and to some extent by choice; a short man who runs emphasizes the shortages of the steps. He hated above all to be hustled and harried by his own emotions.

It was his idea of courtship—if courting was what they were doing—that it should be slow, slowly pacing unstrained, gradually evolving. Perhaps some Castilian strain of his mother's, surviving within him, made him think of the act of getting married as an act of selection among young women you had grown up knowing or knowing of; perhaps there lurked in him a fundamental surprise that he hadn't married any of the girls he had grown up with, but who he had slipped by or who had slipped by him.

He thought there was a deep and basic courtesy in Lee's avoidance of any appearance of hurrying him toward decision—a refinement and distillation maybe of her plains tradition of hospitality. It went against her grain to put a man out of doors before he was ready to go. But, in her tradition, hospitality established counter-claims of courtesy and hospitality. He began arranging for her to meet his friends of long standing, of his own age. Besides being an act of courtesy to Lee, this was a matter of self-interest—he was curious to see how she mixed with them. He was disappointed and annoyed, but in the last analysis not entirely surprised, to see that they regarded her as an amusement of his. Their politeness to her was impeccable; their manner to him was of unexpressed congratulation—if she'd been a little more in their own style, would the congratulations have been unexpressed?—but behind the facade, he saw, amusement lurked. The men, home on leave, sitting with Edwards in chairs beside a swimming pool, drinks in their hands, eyeing Lee's figure on the diving board, watched her with a frank and speculative interest they'd never have allowed themselves if they had thought Edwards was seriously interested in her. If it was a young woman who sat beside Edwards, she praised Lee's looks, in the wicked, knowledgeable and amused tone of an older sister who'd heard of the disreputable circumstances in which the highway patrol recently discovered her little brother in the back seat of a parked car. Edwards' friends of his own generation were married, almost to a man, and a woman. Very few of their marriages had gone bad; the war often had preserved them if only by keeping husband and wife apart. This universally and widespread success of marriage disposed them inevitably and increasingly to think of Edwards as slightly a failure, as somewhat deprived; to minimize any sexual triumphs he might achieve.

His friends' response to Lee made Edwards wary of letting her mingle much with his parents. He took her a few times for drinks at their Pacific Avenue apartment. It was large, rambling, high-ceilinged old place, in a building whose address was much better than its condition. The Edwards' had moved there in the depression, to save money, after selling their town house. (You wouldn't have thought such a house would sell at such a time; the genuinely moneyed, however, always can afford to take advantage of a bargain, which the house

seemingly was. The buyers though, had failed to fore-
see—no one could have foreseen, in those years - that a
fundamental change in their circumstances soon to take
place: the race of servants was to disappear into the
national past, in the unlikely company of the tribal
Indian and the buffalos, making it almost impossible to
maintain such a house.) Garrison and Louise never had
been able to face up to the effort of moving, for the second time and into some other place, all the litter and
memorabilia left by two generations in the four-storied,
half-timbered house Edwards' grandfather had built in
1902.

Reminders of the expansive life Edwards' parents
had lived in the 1920s were all around them—in the
pages of a book, for instance, in Garrison's library, out
of which you might extract a postcard, from Sally (who
had she been?), dated 1927, saying she'd seen Grace and
Jerry in Antibes, and they were all coming home on the
Paris, because the *Ile* was booked full. In the library, too,
was a photograph taken around 1910 of Edwards'
grandfather, who had served as chairman of the San
Francisco police commission, standing on the steps of
the city hall with other members of the commission and
a fine assortment of Keystone Cops: automatically one
peered into the picture, looking for cross-eyed Turpin.
There was another photo of Edwards' grandfather,
standing over a dead lion in the manner of Theodore
Roosevelt (a comparison Edwards' grandfather secretly
may have made); and a photo of Edwards' father as a
young man at the tiller of a sailboat, in the manner of
Franklin Roosevelt (a comparison Edwards' father certainly never made).

When Edwards had taken Margaret there for
drinks he'd been at pains to keep the key low and the
significance muted. He had introduced her as Mrs.

The Duration

Reynolds. Margaret had mentioned "my husband" just the right number of times. Louise had asked, blandly and kindly when he was coming home, which Edwards thought was malicious of her. Both his mother and his father seemed to like her. Nearly every weekend, Margaret and he would stop by the apartment for a drink, or maybe lunch on Sunday. An advance in the state of Louise's knowledge became apparent when she asked Margaret, telephoning her without consulting Edwards to have dinner with them one evening. It was taken for granted by both ladies, during this conversation, that Edwards would be present for dinner: Margaret couldn't escape a feeling that she was being made part of a conspiracy to corrupt Edwards or at least to manage him or turn him back into something as manageable as a child. This aspect of the invitation upset Margaret so much that she forgot what it was about it which originally had upset her, which was that the invitation had been tendered at all. This cause for distress recurred to her mind when she told Edwards about his mother's telephone call; Margaret grimaced then shrugged—she hadn't known she had so many scruples to get rid of.

Louise developed what to uneasy Edwards looked like an attitude of rakish camaraderie with Margaret, who seemed quickly to shed her initial disquietude at this motherly complaisance. Edwards hated to see them go off together into another room, as he sat talking with his father after dinner. They would be gone for a long time. Edwards unhappily imagined his mother telling Margaret the details of some escapade of his younger days. He'd never thought of his mother as having such lapses, but her behavior now made him wonder. He was surprised to find out that, on evenings when he was working, his mother and Margaret sometimes had long

[146]

telephone talks. Next, he thought, they'll be exchanging recipes. He discovered they were.

His parents said little when Margaret no longer appeared in his company. Their tact was enormous — as massive as the tact of nations, which almost never are tactful, but take pains when they are to see that everybody knows about it. When Edwards made up his mind to drop in at his parents' with Lee he wished that he had been there, in the interregnum, with some other girl for cocktails; if he'd done that, Lee's appearance on the scene would have been less of an occasion. Louise flashed a glance of summary appraisal over Lee. After that she was very charming to both of them as if they had just arrived from a defeat, which she had read in their faces.

Edwards felt washing over him gallons of motherly malice, perhaps distilled as a product of her displeasure at his success in seducing Margaret — a displeasure he knew existed, however well she might disguise it; what he didn't know was whether it sprang from outraged propriety or outraged proprietorship. Her manner both to him and to Lee would have seemed to a stranger, unexceptionable. To Edwards she was as jovial as an M.F.H.'s mother at a hunt breakfast; only he could hear in her tone a mocking echo of the manner adopted by mothers who are facing up to the fact their son never is going to amount to much. Talking to Lee she managed to convey at the same time that she recognized that Lee's clothes probably came from and that she never had heard of Neiman-Marcus.

Edwards was surprised to find that Lucius concurred in his mother's judgment that Lee represented a comedown for him. Edwards observed two or three times, after Lee had been out on a story which Lucius had covered too, that Lee later mentioned having seen Lucius but Lucius said nothing to him about having run into Lee. If they saw Lucius in Malloy's after work, he had a drink with them and was pleasant to Lee, but his manner remained abstracted, as if he were listening to music offstage, or for the phone to ring with a message for him from his household in Los Altos or for vibrations in Los Altos. On these evenings he never stayed long in the bar.

Lucius had relished Margaret. It was a sign of how much he thought of her that he'd never proposed that he photograph her. He was always offering to take pictures of Edwards' girls. He made the suggestion in two manners. One conveyed that he was glad to do a favor for Edwards, his highly-esteemed friend. The other implied that he was glad to do a favor for the girl, and was hopeful that she would do one for him. He was a different man with Margaret: courteous, affable and genuinely admiring as a Spanish envoy trading banter with Elizabeth I, with sometimes that flash of something else underneath: sometimes he showed a flicker of jealousy over Edwards' good luck; so small a flicker though that it wouldn't have showed up if he had made a print of his emotions. It was possible that, as with Louise, Lucius was releasing stored-up malice in letting Edwards see that he felt his friend's new choice diminished him. Edwards didn't think so. He believed he detected a sadness in Lucius, the sadness of a man who has seen a good friend let the chance of a lifetime slip from him and now is afraid for his friend's future.

Lee moved among these currents and hostilities as indifferent to them Edwards thought as the hero of a Western, film to the perils of an Indian encampment in which he finds himself: tolerant of its inhabitants' fierce traditions and taboos, confident that he possesses the horse and the horsemanship to gallop easily out of their reach if they turn nasty. Increasingly he admired her.

[TEN]

The old Underwoods, cranky and indestructible, clacked and clattered away: to stop and listen and think of all the nerve ends in fingers jarring fast and hard against those stiff old keys was to receive a cumulative sensation that was like hitting a cast-iron pipe with a hammer. Phones rang and reporters hurrying to finish stories, twenty minutes before deadline, picked them up with crisp annoyed swoops. The desk men threw edited stories into the basket and shouted: "Copy!" At slack times they liked to shout, to goose the single copy-girl reading or woolgathering on the copyboys' wooden bench; but now their voices had an edge, as if they were telling a raw platoon to go over the top, and the girls leapt from the bench like retrievers. The scene had the intensity of a room where bets are being placed. Edwards' phone rang and he picked it up.

Margaret said: "John?"

Overhead, where frantic dust eddied in the harsh

bright lights that hung on long cords from the ceiling, possibility exploded, like a star shell. He said, carefully, "Yes, Margaret."

"I wanted to see you," she said, as if explaining a conversation they'd had earlier. "I have something important to talk to you about." She paused, evidently listening to her own tone, which was distraught; perhaps the realization struck her that he might infer pregnancy. "I think it's important," she said. "Could I see you this evening?"

"Sure, Margaret," he said, still carefully.

"At six? In the little bar in the Stewart?"

The bar was the Highland Room; she knew it was the Highland Room; but some shred of her convent upbringing made her unwilling to acknowledge knowing the names of bars.

"That'd be fine, Margaret," he said.

"I'll see you then, John." Her voice was: excited? Humble? Grateful? He thought so; the descending light of the star shell showed his own figure, clutching a winning ticket to the Irish Sweepstakes.

He looked at the story in his typewriter and decided it could end where it was. Then, in the great tradition of sweepstakes winners who announce they'll use the money to pay off the mortgage and that they'll be staying on the job with J.C. Penney Co., he wrote two more paragraphs before he turned the story in.

He began some rewrites, his last chore of the day. He had finished two before it occurred to him that he must call Lee. He hoped she would be out of the *Binnacle* office. He would have to call her later, at the bar where they met each night; but the time and place of the call would convince her that he was under the stress of an emergency; she'd never guess at deception. He seldom had disliked himself more than after reasoning out this piece of low cunning. She answered her phone. He heard at the wire's other end, the old Underwoods clacking, the phones ringing, the desk men shouting. As he talked the noise dwindled; deadline was past.

"Mother called" he said. "They want me to have dinner with them tonight. Some kind of a family gathering. I may call you when it's over, but it'll probably run late. It's something about my grandmother's estate, which is nothing but goddamned complicated."

He wondered if there had been half-conscious purpose in his choice of excuse. He had been unable not to see lately that Lee resented the slightness of her contacts with his family—resented them as a girl and specifically as a ranch girl to whom the open threshold was sanctified. Lee liked the press parties thrown by large corporations or advertising agencies.

"Free-loader" was a phrase that never would have crossed her mind as applying to herself; she simply was enjoying hospitality, which it was one's right to receive and one's duty to extend, so she had been brought up.

Was he sowing annoyance, half-intending to ease the blow that might be coming to her?

But she said only, "O.K., darling. I'll see you."

He hung up, suddenly aware of the even and industrious typing—too even and industrious, for this relaxed time of day, just after deadline - of the reporters who sat on either side of him, a tough girl and a broken-down public relations man who had got on the staff only because of the manpower shortage. Their devotion to duty must mean that they'd been listening to his successive conversations with interest.

They hardly could think more poorly of him than he thought of himself, still... "Oh, God," he said, to indicate he was a nice guy with problems, not a bastard soaked in duplicity. The tough girl smiled.

The Duration

At five-twenty-five he went to the men's room where he headed for the mirror. A rewrite man came in. He was a Jew of about fifty who assaulted his type-writer with two stabbing forefingers: with the latent fury with which some mammals rut and some birds feed. He was a very fast rewrite man and even a pretty fast typist.

He urinated and remarked: "A great pleasure."

He must have felt a vibration, for he turned around and looked at Edwards, then said amiably: "Oh, well. You're twenty-seven."

Edwards washed his hands, studying his appearance in the mirror; he took a paper towel and scrubbed a carbon paper smudge from his cheek. He washed his hands again. He adjusted the set of his tie. Very few people ever saw him busied like this. His relationship with mirrors was secretive and sexual. Ordinarily he passed them as a man would pass, in the street a married woman he was not supposed to know but had slept with an hour before. As an adolescent he had stood before his bathroom mirror, naked and in profile, admiring his phallic span. Now he did not like to be seen before a mirror doting on his face.

He took the elevator down and went out into the street through the cigar store, off the lobby, where two sports writers were shaking dice with the man behind the counter with an intensity that angered him by its indifference to his troubles. He had four blocks to walk and half an hour to kill. He walked up to Powell Street and went into a bar at random. The drink did him good — not because it was a drink, but because it calmed him to stand there and appear in the mirror behind the bar (there was no harm in using a mirror if you hardly could avoid looking into it) and in the eyes of the bartender as a placid man having a quiet drink at five-

forty-five. He walked out of the bar like a man with far
fewer worries than any of the drinkers who remained
behind.

He had meant to reach the Highland room a few
minutes before Margaret, as a matter of manners, but
she was there first. His heart began to beat insanely as
if its reasons had cost it its reason. She was sitting in a
booth; the room was dim. He saw, as he walked toward
her, that her eyes appeared enormous. As a child he had
seen a mother cat look at him like that from the depths
of a closet where she was nursing her kittens—pleased
to see him, rippling with sensuality, but a little uncertain of his intent, a little apprehensive of his clumsiness.
He looked at Margaret and saw—he thought he saw—
that she had come back to him. They did not say hello;
he slipped, with an air of triumph and ease, into the
seat beside her. At close quarters with her now, he studied her face, remembering the texture of her wide
mouth, remembering an array of sensations. She looked
back at him, kindly reading his thought, but still motherly: then the air between them blurred and sang, and
her mouth fell open, as if for a kiss. To calm himself, he
took inventory of her clothes as she sat there shyly—
neither of them had spoken yet.

He discovered that he knew everything she was
wearing—her wool coat with a fur collar, her cashmere
sweater, her tweed skirt. He craned under the table to
look at her shoes; she looked frightened, then the corners of her mouth twitched with humor—she recognized that she was being checked out, in some way. Her
appurtenances, purse, cigarette lighter, the brand of
cigarette she smoked, were unchanged too. He liked
this—it argued fidelity. In another, more easily committed girl—just such a girl as Margaret wasn't, he hastily
told himself—such an apparent disinterest in new

clothes might simply have meant she'd been so occupied with a man she hadn't had time to care about how she looked when she was dressed. In another girl — and he could tell himself with greater assurance that Margaret wasn't this type of girl — to wear familiar clothes might even have been a subtle taunt, suggesting to him that, what once was his now was somebody else's, that what once had been taken off for him now was taken off for another man. But too it made Margaret seem diminished and pathetic, as if she had been too downhearted or down on her luck to buy new clothes.

A small Filipino waiter stood before them. He was almost exactly the size of General Romulo, whom Edwards had interviewed a few days before, but looked more like a general than Romulo — like a corrupt general, a war lord. He had taken their orders for drinks many times. The appearance on the scene of a third person made Margaret draw away from Edwards — not physically, but he could feel it. At this stage of their encounter with no word yet spoken, any clouding over on her part was enough to panic him — to make all his weather stations report the coming of a new ice age. Perhaps that exchange of lustful looks had been only an indulgence when she had allowed him, allowed herself for old time's sake. Probably he had been over-sanguine; probably she had some commonplace reason for seeing him — had found a book of his in a drawer maybe, and taken the opportunity of assuring herself that she was cured of him.

He looked sideways at her. "Scotch and soda?" he asked, (breaking their silence at last). He spoke neutrally, avoiding the appearance of invoking their old knowledge of one another, trying too to keep out of his voice any implications that time had passed, and her

The Duration

taste, in drinks or men might have changed for the worse.

She hesitated—as if her taste *had* changed. "Yes, please," she said finally, politely, but ending on a note of slight haughtiness if he had presumed.

The Filipino looked puzzled—she always drank scotch and soda—then wise as he moved away.

"He..." Margaret began then stopped.

She took a cigarette from her pack, slowly and with an air of feeling for it in the dark. He lit it: they both did this as badly as if they were a boy and girl in a parked car lighting a cigarette after their first kiss. Edwards saw this resemblance, and flared into silent rage against Margaret, for dragging him back into the humiliations of adolescence which he remembered with Dickensian loathing—hard times wasn't the word for it. At least this business with the cigarette helped to fill the time until the Filipino came back. They seemed in silent agreement that whatever was to be said could be said only after a taste of whiskey.

The drinks came, and Margaret took a gulp of hers. "Ah," she said, and reached for Edwards' hand. They exchanged looks of victory and understanding. They sat, drinking whiskey and holding hands, looking like a married couple who had just played a particularly dirty trick on someone else and were happy about it. Their talk was small talk.

In the night she said, "I dreamed you died. Three nights ago." Fear lingered in her voice.

Her Irish side had taken over, he thought. The fog outside her window had blown in from the Atlantic and the wails that could be heard in it had once been heard in bogs.

But he felt chilled enough wondering what he would say if she got it into her head to ask him where he had been three nights ago. Much worse was the thought of what he would have to say to Lee. To tell her appeared to him as dirty a job as he'd ever undertaken. It was true that there was nothing for which he could be formally reproached, by himself or by Lee. She knew about Margaret.

He'd started once to tell her the bones of the story, feeling he owed it to her, but she had interrupted him, gently, telling him by her tone that she knew all about it or nearly all about it. "I saw you with her once, in the Cirque Room," she said. Edwards was glad to let it go at that.

Lee must have known that the possibility of his going back to Margaret existed; probably she had been in a better position than he to appraise that likelihood; probably in the months just past, she had been better informed than he about Margaret's status, activities and visible state of mind; a woman's lines of communication usually cover more terrain than a man's (besides, he had preferred not to hear news of Margaret).

He'd made no pledges to Lee; had not spoken of love; had not spoken of marriage. Commitment, however, is not merely verbal. She wouldn't have missed the point of those screening visits paid on his parents, his friends. A pleasant complicity had been growing between them, resembling the complicity which existed before they went to bed. To deny this, shatter it overnight at another girl's nod, was hardly less brutal than to leave Lee standing alone at the altar; in a way, it was a more contemptible betrayal, because done privately, not openly and boldly.

And, even dizzied by tonight with Margaret and the thought of more nights to come, he felt a miserly or prudent regret, a quick stab of anguish, at the thought of never holding Lee's whiteness in his arm's again. It could be arranged of course. He must tell her as soon as he decently could, upon seeing her, but even after that, he thought, she probably wouldn't deny him one more night. It might be the best thing he could do for her; to make her a present of some contempt for him. But Margaret would know, and would not forgive him. He had too much to forgive himself for, as it was.

Nobody really believes that all's fair in love and war, he thought; what makes both so dangerous is that their nature forces the use of cruelty even on the few people who aren't cruel, and justifies cruel practice by the rest of us.

Warriors and maybe lovers too, a short, blue-eyed Saxon stock, took Britain from Arthur's people. Saxon Edwards, uneasy in the arms of Arthur's sister, spent a Celtic night filled with guilt, remorse, and telling-over of his own shortcomings and weaknesses.

"You look terrible," Margaret said, with satisfaction, in the morning. "Are you all right?" she laughed.

The moment couldn't have been worse chosen which may have been what stiffened him to take the plunge, feverish with the thrill of peril.

He turned around from the mirror in which he had been looking. "Margaret," he said, "There's this other girl."

She listened with a social worker's air, faintly disapproving and clinical. She wanted to know if Lee were good in bed and he thought she even would have liked details.

The setting, Margaret's shabby little apartment, seemed sordid and depressing to him. He'd become used to the relative splendor of Lee's rooms. Margaret was wearing a dressing gown he knew very well. He had loved to see her in it, because it was what she had put on the first time he had seen her rise naked from her

[157]

bed. Now be noticed only that it wasn't getting any newer. For an instant he wondered if really he liked Lee better. He told Margaret he wanted only her.

In the end she said, kindly enough, "You mustn't blame yourself — it was my fault, really. But you have to see her and tell her tonight. You can call me if you like, when you've told her, but I don't want to see you tonight. Not tomorrow night either. Call me Thursday morning."

He spent the day alternately waiting for Lee to call him and for himself to call her. Finally she called. She was affectionate; her voice had taken on the terrible unawareness of a victim.

He waited until they were in her apartment to tell her. there was some petty caution involved — he didn't think she would cry or curse him, but he wasn't sure. She might throw things — there was violence in her. But beyond this prudence there was an odd scruple at work — he had been reunited with Margaret in a bar, at just this hour, so he felt he owed it to Lee to have their scene in some other setting.

He spoke sparely and economically, in one-sentence paragraphs, like an editorial by the Chief. He wouldn't have believed that her white face could turn whiter. She also became more Western. She walked to her little bar, taking a rider's stiff-legged steps, and poured herself a long drink of straight bourbon. She drank it leaning against the bar, eyeing him with a kind of angry speculation. He saw that her stance was the posture of an injured comrade, not of an injured woman. Now he understood fully why he had such a keen sense that his own behavior had been low. To damage a lover is almost inevitable, but to injure a friend is an indictable offense.

He saw that she was going to suffer more than he had expected. His mind instantly shied away from this, and pounced mockingly upon the fact that her plains accent had become more pronounced.

"Well, John," she said, "We've got no claims on one another." Her drawl had become so noticeable he seemed to hear "I reckon" hang silently in the air at this sentence's end.

She shook herself and said flatly: "You better collect your clothes and things."

Nobody likes to be evicted. Edwards moved around the apartment, collecting shirts, swim trunks, a spare toothbrush and razor. He hesitated as he passed a table on which a book he'd lent her was lying but decided to leave it.

"Don't forget your book," she said.

She sat drinking bourbon and staring out her big window at the waterfront as dark came down over the piers and ships. She seemed to soften a little toward Edwards.

"I'm not angry at you, John," she said. "Don't think I'm throwing you out."

At the end, though, when he stood on the landing in front of her apartment's door, a pile of clothing in his arms, he felt the temptation of pushing him down the stairs shoot through her.

She slammed the door.

A door on the next landing opened and a fat young woman looked out. She was one of the building's ten-ants who had looked at him as if they suspected him of being a leech on Lee. With interest, she watched this confirmation of her theory and what she took to be his expulsion from Eden, for the duration of his trip down the flights of stairs. She was still in her doorway when he came back to pick up the clothes he'd dropped.

Two nights later he was with Margaret. They were subdued. Edwards thought at first that it was only Lee who had cast a shadow over them. Then he saw that the seventy-two hours they had spent apart had been very damaging. They both had too much time to think; they had lost their only hope of recapturing some of the freshness of their early love. In those seventy-two hours, Margaret in her thoughts had denounced him for infidelity. Surely he could have contented himself with casual lays; to find another girl so quickly was an insult to herself, Margaret thought angrily, it cheapened what she had given him. She could hardly have been more indignant if it had been her virginity she had presented to him, and in a way it had been: it is more irrevocable to sleep adulterously with another man than to sleep with your husband.

In his thoughts, Edwards ridiculed the accusation he knew she was levying against him. On both sides, old grievances had been summoned up, old perceptions of the other's shortcomings revived the hostility that always had smoldered, somewhere within each of them had been fueled.

They tried hard. Margaret assured him that as soon as Harry came home she'd tell him their marriage was over. Edwards believed her. She believed herself. They talked about where they would live and the furnishings they would buy. Margaret said she would return to Harry's family the heirloom silver tea set his mother had given them as a wedding gift; then she giggled and said maybe she'd keep it, as having earned it. Harry had lost his sting; they could treat him as a joke.

Margaret went so far as to tell Edwards' parents, one evening after three martinis, that she and John were to be married. The elder Edwards were gravely congratulatory. Edwards thought the congratulations were truly meant, but he also thought Louise doubted that Margaret was as committed as she said she was. Her ear had caught, as Edwards' ear had, the note of strain in Margaret's avowal: Margaret was forcing herself onto a limb, in the hope that it would be sawed off, or was hoping that speaking her wish outloud would give it the force of a reality so real that even time couldn't tamper with it. She was trying to deny herself any options, to foreshorten the future: to put Harry in the position of rebelling against what was ordained and established, and herself in the position of having lived through her difficulties and not being required to do anything further about them.

They fought, each of them, against a sad certainty that these were their last days together. Perhaps in the unconscious belief that a change of scene might do something for them, Edwards tried to collect enough black market gas coupons to take them the two hundred miles to Carmel and back for a weekend. He was able to scrape together only enough to get to Santa Cruz. They walked on the boardwalk, by the hot dog stands; he thought what a mistake it had been to come here and how little his mistake bothered him, and how little he seemed to care about anything.

They drank a lot in these months.

The increasingly low key of their mood was even more depressing because it ran counter to the tenor of the times.

The city was confident, vibrant, exultant; it was like a business that had passed through the early stages of success and is ready to move into the world of tycoonery. Army or Navy officers, seen on the streets, had the air of a newly-created vice president as he ushers you into his huge new office; enlisted men looked like a man in a bar on Saturday night who is confident that, without reprisal, he can beat the hell out of anybody who was talking out of turn to him. The war in Europe was over, the end saluted in the United States offhandedly and without much fanfare, as if it were something the nation had grown out of. Men coming back from the Pacific reported seeing harbors that couldn't contain invasion fleets that stretched out of sight. It seemed certain that Harry would come home soon; perhaps to be discharged, perhaps only on leave before the final onslaught of Japan. Margaret reported every alteration in his prospects to Edwards with a kind of dry scrupulousness as if she felt a silent demand from him that she surrender to him the last remnants of her marriage, and was yielding to his wish but without much admiration for it.

But perhaps she didn't tell him all she knew or maybe Harry didn't tell her all he knew, or the Navy didn't tell Harry all it knew. It was Saturday; Edwards was at the office, Margaret was home. She called him in the middle of the afternoon.

"John," she said. "Listen. Don't come to my apartment tonight."

Edwards was silent. She was silent too, to let him know her meaning was the ultimate one.

To show that he understood, he said: "What time did he get home?"

"Ten o'clock," Margaret said, reluctantly, as if naming the time would conjure up for her, and by empathy might conjure up for Edwards too, the morning hour in which she had been stripped, mounted, skewered.

"I can't talk, John," she said. "I told him I had to go out to get some things for dinner."

Edwards would as soon not have known they planned to spend the evening at home. High anguish shot through him as he thought of Harry lolling in bed, waiting for his wife to come home and cater to him.

"Don't worry, darling," Margaret said. "I love you."

He heard nothing until Monday afternoon, when she

called again. Her voice was hurried, intimate, fond. "Don't worry about us," she said. "It's going be all right for us. Just give me a little time. It is going to be all right."

That was the last he heard from her, except that eleven days later she mailed his meat ration stamp book to him. She sent it to the office. Probably she'd forgotten the address of his apartment — she'd never had any reason to remember it — and presumably was in such a hurry to get the ration book out of her own apartment before Harry stumbled on it that she hadn't even stopped to look up Edwards' address in the phone book. Or maybe there was a deliberate ruthlessness at work: by refusing to accord Edwards eyes the tiny intimacy of admitting that she knew his address, she was putting him and herself on notice that she had washed her hands of him.

Edwards, of course, recognized her handwriting, and tore open the envelope. Two cameramen who were passing his desk looked at the ration book with faintly puzzled expressions, but the dark disgruntled girl reporter who worked at the desk next to Edwards' smiled sardonically. She understood.

*   *   *   *   *

Margaret wasn't sure that she was happy with the sunlight. A fog muffled day might have suited her better, she thought; from a gray city they would have crossed the bridge above a gray bay to reach inland sunlight, their cheerfulness rising to new heights as they sped east, leaving murk and chill behind them. But today cheerfulness was everywhere, which suited her too. The bay stretched beneath them, blue and glittering, its dazzling expanse suggesting the slightly menacing purposefulness of a huge and highly-polished piece of

machinery. Near Alcatraz she could see a civilian frivol-
ity of white sailboats. At the Hunter's Point shipyard, to
their right, an aircraft carrier had appeared, overnight,
in the what-without-asking-whither-hurried whence
way of wartime. Seen through fog its curiously-shaped
bulk would have been an apparition; in today's bright
clarity it was merely industrial, more like a factory than
a ship. To leave the city across this bridge — islands,
water, ships below them — had the finality of flying.

Harry had bought a car, and somehow, by invoking
some formidable connections, had obtained a "C" gas
card so that they could drive across the country. His
orders were for Norfolk. He was pleased because they
would be not far from his home in the Eastern Shore. It
never had occurred to him that after the war he and
Margaret would live anywhere else: he never had asked
if she wanted to live in the Eastern Shore. She was content to have it so. She was glad that she could sit a horse
creditably. She saw herself in a pink coat; more exactly,
she saw herself, pink-coated, with other pink-coated
and handsome people pictured in black and white in a
full-page photograph in *Town and Country*.

It would be a long way from San Diego...oddly
enough, she didn't feel that it was San Diego she would
have come a long way from. She had had a happy childhood in San Diego. She felt that it was Edwards she was
leaving behind in every sense.

Daily he became more diminished. In her mind's
eye he drooped in every attribute.

Harry was looking, with concern it seemed, in the
rear view mirror. She was seized by a sudden fear that
Edwards was pursuing them. She looked around hastily. It was only a highway patrol car.

Frowning, as if reminded of a duty, she began to
think about Edwards. She thought: he must be suffer-

ing, and I'm sorry for that. She thought: he should have known I'd go back to Harry; I'm a married woman, she thought, whatever happens to John, he'll never be a bachelor again.

Ahead of them and below, where the bridge ended on the Oakland salt flats, she could see the tollgates. They seemed a frontier; once they had been passed, she would be exonerated of responsibility for Edwards.

The car ran down the bridge's final glide and onto the salt flats: the earth made itself felt beneath their wheels; it was, a little, like landing in a plane. Most drivers, when they reached the flat, speeded up slightly, as if reassured by the contact of earth. Margaret had the strongest possible sense of returning to the mainland. She felt that she had been on an island adventure. People weren't responsible for what they did when they were shipwrecked to stay alive; the sailors rescuing them didn't ask too many questions. She believed, that Harry must know, at some level of his mind, what had happened to her. He was asking her to act the part of a Bourbon, to pretend that she had learned nothing and forgotten nothing.

The car passed into the toll plaza. Harry gave the attendant a fifty-cent piece and got a quarter back. The whole transaction took hardly fifteen seconds, but in that time Margaret moved closer to Harry and leaned slightly against him. It was a movement of gratitude, as if he had bought her freedom.

The car rolled forward again and Margaret moved gently away from Harry, as if breaking from a kiss and settled contentedly back in the seat for the long journey across the continent with her husband, with whom she would sleep every night of the trip but in a different city, in a nationwide celebration of fidelity, solidarity and sexuality.

[165]

[ELEVEN]

On the evening of August 14, 1945, Edwards went to a party given by a young couple in their Pacific Heights apartment. Husband and wife had been acquaintances of Edwards' at Stanford. Being asked to this party by the Leamingtons, though he hadn't seen much of them in the past three years, was typical of a certain, delicate consideration with which Edwards, these days, found himself being treated by his friends, even those to whom he'd never been especially close. It was comforting, of course, but also slightly comic to him; his friends saw themselves as gently urging him back into the fold. He knew that his male contemporaries, also coming home from the war and beginning to settle comfortably into their professions or family businesses, thought him odd and misguided to have become a newspaperman: a badly-paid trade, which had about it some taint of the menial and subservient, and hadn't yet quite got free from the disdainful old terms; scribbler, snooper. To have involved himself in a dubious affair—adultery of course didn't shock his friends, but the extent of his commitment to it did—and, in an emotional disaster probably seemed to his friends only the predictable consequence of his choice of career. Edwards was a likable man, and his friends' concern for him had some true benevolence in it (though the Leamingtons, for instance, wouldn't have wanted to have Edwards as a guest if he had been visibly sick and sore and sad; misery may love company but company never has returned the sentiment). But also at work was an ancient instinct which refuses to believe in the possibility of a classless society, and puts a good deal of faith in numbers: one more defender to man the ramparts if the peasants should rise, is worth having. (And who can say that this instinct is entirely far-fetched? Who can say that the Hundred Minutes War won't produce another jacquerie among the survivors? Somebody will have to be blamed.)

When a stray is welcomed back, naturally there is a certain amount of curiosity about what he has strayed into. Edwards' friends were too well-mannered to refer to his trouble often, but they also were too well-mannered never to mention it: they would not tiptoe around his disaster. The men were hearty and forthright ("Her husband came home, I hear") if they found themselves alone with Edwards, drinking in a club bar or in a corner at a party; they laughed, and patted him on the back; it might be bovine, but it had herd comfort in it. The wives managing to discover themselves isolated with Edwards in a kitchen or by a swimming pool, showed, a bright eager curiosity about the details of what had happened. Their interest appeared more sisterly or cousinly or kissing cousinly than purient; they seemed to say unspokenly that Margaret must have been in the wrong and couldn't have been good enough for him anyway; after all, if they hadn't met Tom or Jack just at the time when Edwards was going out with Helen, who knows?

Though he was grateful for their kindness, Edwards cherished some resentment toward his friends because of their attitude toward his trade. He thought they were mistaken: that a good deal of power and even some money lay ahead of him. The desk already had suggested to him, in barroom conversations late at night or when stalling off a request for a raise, that he might go a long way in the national chain of which the *Observer* was a part, "if you stick with us," this last being accompanied by a searching look; always the doubt whether he wasn't only a sojourner, a dilettante, a scion of empire working in the colonies for kicks or until something better turned up. But, as he began to move up into the hierarchy, the traits and manners which now made him suspect would sometimes, and increasingly, be an advantage. Besides, life is a long patrol in enemy territory. If you survive, you develop increasing respect for the idiosyncrasies of those who survive with you; you imagine, or perhaps see clearly, that the traits which annoyed you in a companion helped keep him alive.

Edwards' Irish superiors—some of whom perhaps were beginning to feel that they might not always be his superiors—would come to accept him as a second lieutenant who continues to live through combat is accepted. Edwards noticed that this process was working upon his friends too. They no longer seemed quite so sure it was faintly embarrassing of him to have decided to be a newspaperman. His friends were still young enough to be impressed by the fact that he had met and talked with the Missimo and Averell Harriman and Wendell Wilkie, on the often surprisingly equal terms his profession made possible. He was a man who could fix parking tickets — this appealed to friends of all ages, from sixteen up.

As the friends of his own generation grew older, they became increasingly appreciative of the advantage of knowing a man who might be able to tell you where to go in city hall to make sure of getting a paving contract or to have a few fire regulations overlooked during the inspection of the fifty-year-old mansion you were remodeling into apartments, it meant something to his friends (and why not? We all place our acquaintances by their artifacts and regalia, including what kind of snobbery they wear next to their skins) that, though he had been a newspaperman for five years, they still ran into him buying shirts at Bullock and Jones or having his hair cut by Fritz in the Palace barber shop, or vacationing in Santa Barbara. It unsettled them to see him calm and smiling and accustomed, in such surroundings, gave them an uneasy feeling that he was on to something good — maybe it was just himself — whose significance they had misjudged that was another reason they were unusually kind to him right now. It reassured them to contemplate his amorous debacle; they had been right after all; he was a bit of a fool, or somewhat odd.

Edwards thought that time would prove his friends wrong, and in the meantime he valued their company and could endure their patronage; but his self-esteem was under deeper and subtler assault from another set of shepherds and mentors. He had taken to seeing more of his parents, dropping by the high-ceilinged, labyrinthine, slightly shabby apartment on Pacific Avenue for dinner, even spending a weekend with them in their beach cottage at Bolinas; partly because he had time on his hands and felt he had neglected his parents during his affair with Margaret, partly out of a need to be reassured, to test his familiar relationships as a recovering invalid tests the muscles he formerly took for granted. His father and mother knew, from him, that he and Margaret had broken up, in a final way; they seemed to have picked up some details elsewhere. (Edwards often reflected that Ivan the Terrible, who had messengers bearing bad news nailed to the floor by their feet, didn't go far enough; he should have put his top-seeded sadists to work on the man who *told* the bad news to the bearer of bad news: strike at the people who are so energetic in reporting the misfortunes of others and you'd eliminate a lot of bad news, in every sense, from the world.)

Garrison, who had been so worldly and rueful and gentle about his son's affair with Margaret, so unfailingly courteous to Margaret herself, now had allowed his disapproval of his son's behavior to come out in the open. As a lawyer, he tended to reserve judgment (after all, that wasn't his métier) and to be strongly influenced by verdicts. In the matter of Propriety v. John Edwards, an unmarried man, and Margaret Reynolds, a married woman, a judgment had been handed down, old precedents validated; the scales had come down on the side where he had expected to see them incline and, fundamentally, where he had wanted them to be. He showed how he felt mainly by never mentioning Margaret.

Louise, on the subject of Margaret, was urbane and sensible and even raffish. She didn't attempt to pry information out of Edwards; she seemed more concerned to instruct him about the nature of what had happened. "I feel very sorry for Margaret," she said, finally. "If the war hadn't happened and you hadn't come along she might have had a perfectly good life with her husband. She'll try to settle down with him now, and maybe she will for a while, especially if they have children, but it won't last. You'll be only the first, and she'll get less fastidious about who she goes to bed with, as time goes on. If she does settle down it'll only be after she's forty, and providing her husband puts up with her behavior or doesn't find out about it, which isn't very likely."

These not un-brutal comments were delivered with an antiseptic unsparingness, as if Edwards had them coming to him. But Edwards recognized that his mother, though indulging herself a little in motherly spite, also was wooing his affection, as once she might have wooed him with a trip to the zoo. She was offering him the compliment of declaring belief that Margaret, having known him, would remain dissatisfied with her marriage and would be dissatisfied, among other reasons, because Edwards was a stud. She had implied also that she wasn't affronted — either as a mother according to Hoyle or a mother according to Freud — by his being a stud; Edwards didn't believe this protestation and doubted that his mother believed it. She had added the implication that she even was proud of his potency, which probably was partly true; mother-son relationships seldom are as simple as in the story of Oedipus and Jocasta. At any rate, his mother's commentary was better than moralizing, even silent moralizing of the sort his father was practicing.

These conversations with his mother didn't entirely please Edwards — after all, his sex life wasn't what it had been, and it helped make up the margin, between what he had enjoyed and what he currently could count on, to indulge in these queer verbal titillations — although he sometimes wished afterward that less had been said. He took alarm only when his mother began saying, when one or another of her friends who never had understood the Margaret situation asked him if he were still seeing that charming blonde girl, "I believe John is cut out to be a bachelor." After the third time his mother said this Edwards began bringing Lee, with whom he had patched up matters more or less, around to his parents, for a drink or dinner. Louise correctly read this as tactics; she let Edwards see that she had made a final assessment of Lee as merely a convenience to him, or a saving of his face.

Once, on an evening when Lee wasn't present and his mother had drunk two martinis, she spoke of Lee as "this reprise of yours" — she spoke the word "reprise" with such particular scorn that Edwards had no trouble translating it into the idiom of his own generation, as "retread." She continued to be very charming to Lee.

"Your mother is wonderful, but I incline toward your father," Lee observed tentatively to Edwards, her manner suggesting that she wondered how deeply he was willing to explore the subject of his mother. "You're supposed to; you're a girl," he answered. Both recognized that this answer, though unexceptionably true, was inadequate to the situation: it was like saying that you didn't dine at the Borgia's anymore because you'd been told to watch your diet. Lee had her answer though; she understood that this was an old malaise about which Edwards didn't think anything could be done. She thought he was wrong; like nearly all women she agreed with psychiatry that most situations can be bettered by talking about them, and like nearly all women she went beyond psychiatry by believing that most situations can be made twenty times better by talking them over twenty times; or if not, at least you've had the fun of talking.

Chance had made it so easy for Edwards to pick up where he'd left off with Lee that the very extent of his luck may have made it easy for him to get back in bed with her: luck is the psychic counterpart of brute strength, and a girl who tries to fight off a lucky man soon is overmastered by the pleasant sensation of making a hopeless resistance. They met while out on a story, a fire in the Mission district. The fire amounted to nothing, the time was five in the afternoon; both of them were told, on telephoning in, to knock off for the day. The nearest phone had been in a neighborhood bar. Edwards led the way into the bar, but stood aside to let Lee use the phone first; his expression was faintly ironical; he knew she would have preferred that he outrace her to the phone, conceding nothing to her sex.

She stood by while he phoned, one of those outsize leather bags of hers tucked under her arm; her face reported that she was in a hurry to be off but was not going to be outdone in courtesy. It would have been uncouth of Edwards not to offer to buy her a drink, and of course it was what he wanted to do. She accepted, not making much out of her acceptance; a drink is a drink, her tone commented. She glanced about her as she sat down at the bar and seemed to repeat this observation. The bar was called the Bit of Erin, in the tradition of bars in this part of town. It had been designed by the WCTU; its patrons were from an original idea by James Joyce, with additional dialogue by Nelson Algren.

Behind the plank stood a bartender whose name was Pat or Mike or John L. Sullivan or Niall of the Nine Hostages; red-faced and burly, he eyed Edwards and Lee with the suspicion and disdain of a man who drinks only beer and straight shots, clearly believing that they might be about to order Pimm's Cup. They asked for martinis, which he mixed with as much muscularity as if they had been cake batter; he filled their glasses not quite to the brim and ostentatiously threw out the liquor remaining in the pitcher.

The Duration

"Bastard," Lee observed as the bartender walked away, not quite out of earshot. Edwards reflected that she had the detached air of a girl who doesn't care if her escort does get in a fight. When they met at the scene of the fire her manner had been guarded, although mostly she had been busy covering the fire. She took fires seriously; she took most stories seriously. The battalion fire chief assured her the blaze quickly out, hadn't amounted to anything; so did Edwards (she gave him a distrustful look); so did her photographer, who was in a hurry to get to another assignment; so did her desk, when she called in her report; but still she worried that a story might be eluding her, lost somewhere among the buttes and canyons of male obtuseness.

She remained preoccupied and remote as they sat drinking, Edwards making the conversation, telling jokes, offering gossip, ordering another drink (she had finished hers quickly, with an absent-minded thoroughness). He talked on until, although she still didn't seem to be giving him her full attention, he felt the quality of her preoccupation shift, almost with a click. Instead of staring more or less unseeingly into the mirror behind the bar she lowered her head, the ash blonde hair falling across a cheekbone and hiding an eye, and began to fiddle with an ashtray on the bar. She was the picture of a girl trying to listen to something else — music, maybe — while a man talked her ear off (there was a jukebox, but its music evidently was valued for the degree of healthy competitiveness it made necessary: the bar's customers relished loud tunes they could shout above).

Lee smiled to herself, or she looked mournful. Once she raised her head and looked Edwards in the eyes, with an expression of childish hurt. He gathered that when they sat down to drink she'd assumed that he would try to get her into the hay for the evening, and was prepared to brush him off without undue resentment; she had that placidly of ranch-bred girls, who flick off men as a horse flicks off flies.

Now that she understood that he truly was courting her, that he meant to ask her to come back to him — was asking her already, really, though he'd talked only about casual topics — she was plunged into the state of emotional vulnerability that follows the close of all hostilities. Edwards had asked for an armistice, and like all victors she was exclaiming: what have we done to one another? But she must be counting her casualties too; even to consider the possibility of going back to Edwards would bring to life again the memory of the pain he had inflicted on her. He was making her suffer it all over again, as if he were analyst and he couldn't even claim, as an analyst could, that he wanted her on the couch for her own good (or would he have the nerve?). In fact, he was being truly presumptuous; he was asking her to take him back, he was assuming that she was available and not spoken for, and he was obliging her to undergo the painful quickening into life again of memories she had locked away in some prison camp of her spirit where she allowed them only an occasional Red Cross package of emotion.

So Edwards construed her thoughtful silences. They drank some more; Lee grew cheerful and told him a new verse of "I Used to Work in Chicago" she'd learned, she didn't say where or from whom. Edwards experienced a stab of jealousy, which no doubt Lee had intended him to feel; simultaneously she had invoked their old intimacy and in summoning it up had reminded him that whatever she had done with him she could do with another man.

Six-thirty came and Lee said she must be getting home; Edwards panicked a little and ordered more drinks. Lee smiled, broadly. A younger and friendlier bartender came on shift (the first one had progressed from a contemptuous assumption that they were featherweight drinkers to a censorious implication that they drank too such). "How are you folks, tonight?" he said. "You folks" seemed to draw them together; it was the word for which they'd been waiting, the omen they had lacked. They answered the bartender with disproportionate friendliness; he guessed that they were a couple making up a quarrel.

As a bartender, he often was on the receiving end of this pathetic eagerness to be liked by everybody, which was displayed not by the lost but by the rescued, people who had found or regained an ally and so decided to reopen negotiations with the rest of humanity. He also had been a merchant seaman, in the first days of the war, and had seen the same pathos, the will to love and be loved, in the rescued survivors of torpedoings.

Clamor grew around them. Like all recent arrivals at a tumultuous bar or party, Edwards and Lee had a sense that the situation was rushing past them, expanding past their grasp; they sat at the bar like a schoolmarm from St. Louis and her banker fiancé, waiting helplessly for the moment when the gunfighter would burst through the saloon doors and shoot off both their hats simultaneously, while the crowd ducked and roared. The bar's patrons couldn't have been noisier if they hadn't had anybody but cows to talk to for seven months. Soon, like the ten-gallon hats of riders coming from the range, the helmeted heads of shipyard workers, men and women, began to move through the throng, arriving from Hunter's Point on the other side of town. They at least had the excuse that they'd been shouting all day, if they wanted to be heard, and hadn't had time yet to throttle down to a normal noise level.

The Duration

Edwards and Lee had elbows driven into their sides; demands for drinks were shouted past their ears.

A helmeted man jostled Lee's arm and knocked half her drink from the glass. "Sorry, honey," he said. "Buy this girl a drink," he told the bartender, and instantly turned away from her with the lordly indifference of a man who has seen social justice done in the time, and actually would rather sleep with Mme. Defarge than with the Vicomtesse de Beauharnais.

All this hubbub made it easy for Edwards and Lee. They left the bar not like people who had to reach a decision, but simply as a couple who wanted to escape somewhere and have a drink in peace and quiet: that this was advisable after their hardships never had to be put to the question. If a decision had been made, it had been made for them by other people; the sigh of relief they gave, after they'd bumped and fought their way out onto the sidewalk, were really at having escaped the hard chore of decision and commitment. They allowed familiar rhythms to take hold. To have been delivered from those shouting strangers drew them together, like a married pair leaving a party that they have found harrowing but comic. Lee took Edwards' arm.

"Where's your car?" she said comfortably. Her tone was so easy that its easiness was significant: amused as Mozart at her mastery of her medium, she was telling him that it was Christmas Eve, that Santa Claus hadn't forgotten him, and he would be unwrapping his package before morning.

Later, she took him home and to bed with her, without question or hesitation or stipulation. But in the morning when he wanted to renew—it was an advantage of her coloring that her looks didn't suffer in the morning when she was tousled and not made up; let her hair grow, and find her a big enough sea shell, and she

[177]

could have been as palely, coolly and freshly naked as Botticelli's girl—she got out of bed and said that they both had to get to work. She walked to the bathroom and shut the door behind her with a gentle emphasis: no seal-like sport in the shower this morning. When she came out she was wearing a bathrobe, apparently with nothing on underneath. As she moved around, getting breakfast, he received views of breast and leg revealed to him with a lack of self-consciousness which could have suggested either that he'd ceased to exist for her as a sexual object or that she had accepted him back into an accustomed relationship.

She felt his stares and said, "Don't sulk," John. "There'll be other nights. Other mornings, if that's what you want." But when they were dressed and ready to go she kissed him, then held him at arm's length and looked in his face as she said: "You've got to understand that things are different, John."

A flick of triumph showed in the pale eyes. He soon found out what she meant. That afternoon he called her and asked if he could buy her a drink after work.

She said, coolly that she wouldn't be able to see him. He waited two days and called again. This time she said, but still coolly, "Yes, I'd like to."

She smiled warmly when she saw him, and took his arm: he thought it was one of those smiles with which women announce that a relationship has been stepped up, or an old intensity resumed. Actually, it meant only that she felt easy and kindly because she had made up her mind to a course of action. That night in bed, as they lay relaxed, she said, "John, I won't be able to see you every night."

"I see," he said.

She lay passive, her eyes closed. Her message was delivered; it was up to him to decide what happened next. After a while he rolled on top of her. She met his strenuous thrusts with fierceness and scratchings. This was something new. A store of malice was being released. She gave him, as it were, blow for blow; and as she relished each stroke she defied him to find out how he measured up to her new standard for comparison.

Edwards didn't like the way in which she had got such complete control of the situation. He thought things over for two days, and then called her again. As a reasonable man he had to acknowledge her right to score some points at his expense; as a humorous man he was wryly amused at her manner of managing to do so; and as a sensible man he told himself he would be foolish to deprive himself of an available (if not always) and excellent lay. Besides, though not everybody is a glutton for punishment, everybody has some appetite for it. Since childhood he had not been dominated by a woman. To let Lee have the upper hand of him, to the extent that she did, was a mild form of indulging in a dubious and dangerous pleasure (like smoking pot but stopping at that).

Sometimes she teased him by leaving something around in plain sight in her apartment which obviously had been left behind by the other man (a tie) or which would make Edwards guess (a masculine-looking cigarette lighter). Edwards said nothing and soon was able not even to seem to notice. She never spoke of the other man and Edwards didn't ask questions. Sometimes he wondered how she accounted to the other for the nights she spent with Edwards; perhaps the other man had another girl? *Quelle ronde.* They never mentioned Margaret either, though Lee managed to give the impression that she could bear to talk about Margaret, but doubted that Edwards could.

The Duration

Generally speaking they were back on their old terms of easy good humor, though now it had a touch of contempt on both sides. They could afford this, because they had no future. Contempt always is in order when a love affair has foundered in shallow water, before really making sail: blame rests with the one who was at the helm, but his crewman must have been inept too.

It was noticeable that now, when they discussed the war Lee often challenged his views. He supposed this was partly to let him know that he had been diminished in her eyes and partly because she was receiving opinions from another man.

They argued on the evening of August 6. Lee maintained that the bomb which had been dropped on Hiroshima wasn't going to end the war. "It's been proven," she said.

"Bombing cities just doesn't have much effect."

Edwards deduced that at least the new man had nothing to do with the Army Air Corps.

"So it's a bigger bomb," Lee said.

It was, Edwards later supposed, something to remember; his first argument, with so many to come, about the atom bomb.

On August 13 the word was that President Truman would speak to the nation by radio the next day, presumably to announce the war's end. That night there was a lot of drinking, but not much celebration. In the downtown streets, the enlisted men smashed windows and were high-handed to some degree with people they had resented—officers, civilians and girls—jostling them, slapping them familiarly on the back, forcing swigs from bottles of them, kissing them. They had risen against the city. Aside from this special case, the city's mood was much like that of a man who has gone through a lot to get a woman and now isn't sure he wants her. The future had arrived, unexpectedly soon, and was at everyone's throat.

Edwards thought, in a couple of bars that he visited with Lee before they went to her apartment, that it was like New Year's Eve; there was hysteria in the gaiety professed because a milestone was about to be reached, though not everyone was glad to see it come. In Lee's apartment they drank quietly and for a long time, looking down at the dark waterfront that would be bright tomorrow night.

"I suppose they'll turn the lights on tomorrow night," Lee said suddenly.

Step by step, each one in the city was arriving at his own realization of all that was about to happen.) They went to bed and made a little boozy love. In the middle of the night Lee woke him up. "You were right about the bomb," she said, and went back to sleep.

She said the same thing the next morning as she brought him the morning paper in bed, where he lay hung over. "You were right about the bomb." Either she had been drunker than Edwards realized last night, or she was one of those people who sometimes act in their sleep without remembering. In his spent mood, he felt little curiosity. He didn't have to be at work until ten. Even so, he didn't succeed in permanently getting out of bed until some time after Lee had gone. (She left with a suggestion of hurry, which indicated that she didn't want to be asked if he would see her that night). There wasn't time to go to his own place and change.

He shaved, cleaned and dried the razor with great care—whoever used it next could sneer only at his lack of godliness—sneaked out of the building and caught the Hyde Street cable car. Its teeth-jarring progress was, to a man with a hangover, like being trepanned while

The Duration

the anesthetic was wearing off. Dimly he noticed an occasional bottle in the gutter. They passed a neighborhood liquor store; its window had been smashed and all the bottles on display taken. The bottles in the gutter were thicker as the car approached downtown. The day was clear and bright; the air had a neutral and antiseptic quality. Edwards felt as if the car unopposably rushing downhill were a table on which he was being rolled toward some relentlessly surgical happening.

At Geary Street he got off, with relief, and walked the few blocks to the office. Locomotion restored his sense of being in control of what he was to do next. The windows of all the liquor stores on Geary and down Powell were shattered. All the bottles were gone from the windows, but the stores' shelves were undisturbed. Edwards wondered whether this was from some sense that to take a bottle from the window was privileged frolic while to enter a store and remove one was theft, or simply from a prudent wish not to be caught in a store if the law should arrive. (Where *had* the cops been last night?) It seemed to Edwards that there were unusually few people on the streets. He thought he sensed guilt in the air; it was like coming down for breakfast at a house party where everyone has been very drunk the night before, and finding that no one else has been willing to emerge and face up to the happenings of the night. There was apprehension too; the actual night of victory was yet to come. The bare bright streets might have been in a Latin American capital where gunfire was expected momentarily. Guilt and fear didn't touch Edwards: he moved within his hangover like a man to whom everything already has happened.

At the office it was better. There was a cheerful bustle. The desk men looked pleasantly stimulated, but

[182]

unruffled. A day like this, when a newspaperman can feel that he is presiding over history like a master of ceremonies, reasonably certain that the acts are going to appear as scheduled without causing him any undue strain, is very much to an editor's taste. The deskmen's confident and controlled excitement communicated itself to the city room, increasing the strong sensation that it was Christmas Eve; gifts lay ahead for everybody, though few could be sure exactly what they would be. Christmas is the child of Saturnalia; as the afternoon passed more and more reporters sent copyboys out for Cokes, of the kind which had to be bought at a bar, where the Coke was poured out, a shot of whiskey poured in, and Coke replaced on top of it to fill the bottle again. (Malloy's, which wanted to stay on good terms with the *Observer's* management, refused this trade, but there were less scrupulous bars down the street.)

Although copygirls greatly outnumbered the copyboys, only boys were sent on this errand, except for one notorious copygirl who had so much on nearly everybody anyway that her potential for damage could hardly be increased. Presently somebody took a pint from a desk drawer, took a nip from it and handed it to the man next to him. Soon another pint was circulating. The drinking had to be done in plain view of the city desk, but appearances were preserved by passing the bottles from hand to hand behind the reporters' desks, out of the desk men's view. The drinkers, as they brought the pint down after taking their swigs, glanced quickly at the desk to see how it was taking this. The desk men looked as if they would like a drink themselves. A reporter slyly tested this theory by handing a bottle to one of the rewrite men who helped himself and passed the bottle on to the desk. The assistant city editor took a big swig, as if it were long overdue, but the city editor shook his head. There was an hour to go until deadline.

A copyboy came at the run from the teletype room and handed a yellow slip torn from the machines to the news editor, a youngish red-face man who wore a hearing aid. He read the paper carefully, then — evidently resolved not to break his rule of never shouting as other deaf men did — simply passed the slip across his desk to the assistant managing editor. This man, dark, mustached and flamboyant, had natural immunity against the fear of being obvious.

He glanced at the slip, turned to face the room and bellowed: "It's over!" He looked at the faces turned toward him; perhaps he saw in them an *Is that all?* for everyone in the room had seen the dumb-show and recognized its significance; maybe feeling a little silly, he added, summoning up some inexpensive irony: "Harry says it's over." The inhabitants of Aix, to whom he had brought the news, had no sense of occasion, so he reverted to his newspaperman's stance of judicious skepticism. If anyone had made himself ridiculous, his tone implied, it was Harry Truman.

Edwards thought that it was a long way from the days of Coral Sea and Midway, when men had clustered around the teletypes, haunted by the sense that just possibly they might live to see the Japanese warships, with their fantastic funnels that looked as if they had been trained by patient gardeners to grow into odd shapes, lying at anchor below Goat Island, their guns trained on the city. The city editor reached into his desk and brought out a fifth, which he placed on the desk's edge in easy reach of anyone: license was proclaimed. More bottles appeared; paper cups bloomed.

After the first edition's deadline was past, at four-thirty, only two men in the room remained really industrious. A rewrite man, allowing himself only small and infrequent sips from a paper cup, was shuffling through a pile of clippings; he was writing a long recapitulation of General MacArthur's deeds in this war. At the back of the room the photo editor was sorting his way through hundreds of pictures of MacArthur.

The telephones were not known to have brought any message from the Sierra aerie where the Chief presumably was contemplating the day the Lord had made. No message was necessary; his bailiffs and stewards knew whose name it was up to them to glorify. But maybe there had been a message, for the revelers were startled by the sudden appearance of the publisher, walking as if it were any day, blandly and Jewishly unimpressed by history. His hooded eyes opened a little in surprise at the free-and-easy scene, swept over it and looked away. Edwards had seen almost exactly the same expression on the face of a doctor who had opened the door of a back room in a high school gymnasium and unexpectedly disclosed one of the school's most celebrated athletes: whose sport at the moment was solitary. The publisher stepped neatly to the desk of the assistant managing editor, bent over him and spoke briefly in low tones, then left, his black-clad back as tactful and disapproving as a head waiter's who is walking away from a tableful of drunks. If he had transmitted a message from the Sierra, it may have accounted for some of his attitude of distaste.

The Chief who was the publisher's master might regard General MacArthur as an avatar of his self, to be worshiped as one avatar may worship another avatar, but the publisher was unlikely to have a high regard of the general. The publisher, all smooth surfaces and subdued coloring, was as utterly civilian as a banker, as an undertaker, as a mandarin. If he truly had been a mandarin, in his home's privacy he would have taken his brush and written upon rice paper a poem deploring the brutish necessity of employing generals. Perhaps, in his own family circle, the publisher did something like that; tossing in a few reflections upon emperors.

He passed, self-possessed as an enormous pigeon, out of the doorway, which was the only entrance to the city room. This door, on its other side, was inconspicuous, located behind a metal stairway at the end of a long hall, to keep at a minimum the traffic in interlopers and nuts. As soon as the publisher had gone through the door Lucius appeared in it, camera in hand. Photographers entering the city room and heading for the darkroom at the rear always moved at a trot—not like men who were trying to demonstrate that they were on the job, but like a man who'd carried a valuable load for some distance, and speeds up as he nears his goal, to cut down the time in which he has to worry about dropping it. They carried their cameras high, as if their contents might spill if bumped. This was of course a sensible precaution, to keep the camera from getting smashed in the crush of people in the narrow aisle between the reporter's desks and the copy desk; but few cameramen leaving the room on an assignment kept their cameras as high as the men returning, conscious that they carried something valuable and liable to spoilage.

Lucius went into the darkroom with his holders, and came right out again. (This meant the assignment had been routine; if he had thought the negatives had any claims to merit, he would have souped them himself.) He sat down, companionably, at the desk next to Edwards'. He fitted a cigarette into the holder. His fingers didn't shake, but there was a vibration in the air surrounding them as there is around a phone that is about to ring. Lucius never had developed a full coat of mail against human folly and malice, and the blind malevolence of the universe. These twin sources of peril sometimes mingled; to produce automobile accidents, for instance; Lucius had not been able ever to harden himself against shock when he took pictures of these.

The war appeared to him as an enormous traffic accident. He had managed not to think about it by concentrating on the petty harassments and deprivations it back brought to him, as he might have forgotten about an accident he had photographed by concentrating on the fact that covering it had made him an hour late to dinner; but today, when the war was over, he had to look at it. He said nothing, but smoked while Edwards finished rewriting a release. His hand did shake a little; probably he had a hangover. Edwards finished the story, took it out of the typewriter and said the best thing that could be said.

They stood up and started downstairs for Malloy's. Edwards wasn't supposed to be off for an hour yet; he paused by the city desk and told Jimmy McKeon he'd be downstairs if wanted. McKeon gave him a sharp little glance but nodded. Another man would be coming home from the Army — was rumored already on the way — to take back the chair McKeon sat in. McKeon was on the lookout for any hint of an attempt to flout his dimmed authority.

Malloy's was crowded with men Edwards didn't remember ever having seen before. They were richly dressed by newspapermen's standards. They might be from the Montgomery Street financial houses, having wandered here because they were attracted to power, and a newspaper building on a day of great news seems invested with power. Or they might be from the display advertising staff (which normally shunned this dingy

[187]

bar), salesmen who had voted themselves the afternoon off and were protecting themselves by invoking whatever marginal right they had to be called newspapermen; this was an afternoon for newspapermen to get drunk in a newspaperman's bar, and that was what they were doing.

Whoever they were, they were loud. Malloy stood behind his bar, sweating and uneasy, wincing whenever a glass was dropped. The sound of glass shattering that afternoon in that city where the remnants of panes hung jagged in the liquor store windows, struck the nerves of any bartender as the sight of smoke would affect a forest ranger. One glass broken, like one rape in a just-captured city, might by example set off a whirlwind of terror: in this bar, as elsewhere in the city, a dangerous male excitement was just barely under control, and was being fanned by a sense that today the rules were suspended. The few bottles of good whiskey that remained to Malloy had disappeared from the back bar. Either he believed they shouldn't be wasted on a night when anything with alcohol in it could be sold, or else he was prepared to be sacked.

Bland and resolute, Lucius pushed his way through to a place at the bar. A crowd of rowdy drinkers calmed and steadied him, reinforced in him his sense of his own worth, as some fighting men are calmed and steadied by finding themselves among a rabble of cowards. He meant to drink martinis, and he was not going to have them handed to him from the bar by a fire-bucket chain of shouting drink-sloppers. He would sit gravely at the bar and see the martini mixed before his eyes; judiciously he would watch it as it was poured into his glass. He would contemplate his dividend, as it stood before him in the glass shaker, until he saw the whites of its eyes.

The Duration

Edwards, following in Lucius' wake, had to wait for a seat. There was a vacant stool next to Lucius, but it was blocked by a large bellowing man who stood ordering drinks and passing them to people behind him. After a little while he seemed to feel that his magnanimity wasn't receiving sufficient notice; he collected a lot of drinks and went off to dispense them. Edwards slipped into the seat. He felt, though, that the giant would be back, and he soon was, paying no attention to Edwards and simply ordering more drinks over Edwards' shoulder.

Edwards sat tensed, waiting for a drink to be slopped onto him. Lucius saw his condition, but couldn't say anything; he knew Edwards wouldn't yield so much as an inch of air to a man that big. The large man left again with more drinks; when he came back to the bar, he stood behind someone else. While Edwards' feathers settled into place Lucius puffed on his cigarette holder and sipped his martini, as shrewd and busy as a pasha pulling at his hookah, or Gandhi at his weaving, he seemed to be waiting for Edwards to say, as Edwards soon did: "Shall we get out of here?" It was an afternoon, they clearly were in agreement, for quiet, elegant, rueful, worldly-wise drinking; an afternoon for humanists to indulge in the praise of folly, while becoming as smashed as icons. The clamor around them was all wrong.

They went out of the bar and stared at Market Street, appalled.

They'd come into Malloy's through the alley where the circulation trucks waited, so they hadn't seen what was happening on the city's main street; they'd heard the uproar, though the noise then had been less than it was now, but they were preoccupied with getting to a drink. Once inside Malloy's, the clangor outside was muffled by the hubbub within.

[189]

The Duration

The traffic had frozen, solid, all up and down the broad thoroughfare. The streetcars, four abreast, stood embedded among the automobiles like ships ruefully aground among lubberly barges. Soldiers and sailors, abetted by civilians who looked and acted as if they had emerged from cellars, where they had been conducting a resistance movement, swarmed over the helpless streetcars, stripping their fenders and trolleys from them. The motormen stamped on their bells, as always; but they stamped and jangled as cheerfully as reindeer on Christmas roofs; their mood seemed that of the Cossacks in Petrograd of 1917 genially greeting the people instead of flailing them with knouts.

On the sidewalks enlisted men knocked the hats off officers and kissed officers' girls in a way that stopped short of rape but not short of insult. The officers endured, palely grinning. The street's great lampposts looked as if they were meant to hang the privileged from; and it was true that this street had known violence again and again: tear gas, bombs, gunfire, strewn bodies, grim silent marchers, on a day in 1934 as sullen as any in Petrograd's streets.

Wild girls shrieked through the crowd: bacchantes from behind the counters of dime stores, who before dawn would bathe naked in the staid fountains at the Civic Center, amusing those amorous birds, the civic pigeons.

There was no chance of fording this Mississippi to the other side of Market, where the better bars were. They went back into Malloy's and drank for two hours. Lucius became a little nasty and brought up the subject of Margaret, saying — what Edwards was sure he didn't believe — that maybe it had worked out just as well for everybody. Edwards had been expecting this attack. It was a day for summations and regrets. Lucius was feeling sorry, for perhaps the last time, that he hadn't had Margaret himself. Edwards even welcomed having this knife turned in him by his friend. It was better than doing it later himself, in solitude.

At eight o'clock they parted, in the alley behind the bar, shaking hands, wringing one another's hands, with some emotion — as if, Edwards thought, they were going off to war. Lucius departed to risk his life on the highway to Los Altos, and Edwards made his way across Market, where the traffic jam had thinned out to the consistency it normally had at about five o'clock, and headed for the cable car which would take him home. He thought he might have some trouble as a civilian from the rowdy crowd, but met none. Clearly the distinction had ceased to exist for the men in uniform: they were all civilians. Anyway, the crowd seemed to make way for him as he lurched purposefully along the sidewalk; afterward, thinking about it, he couldn't decide if they had recognized him as a man under a private load of strain or grief, or just as a man with a load. In his apartment he fell onto the bed and slept until eleven, when he woke up dazed and thirsty and in the dark. He had seldom felt so alone.

He had a sense of unidentified loss. He lay thinking and then realized what had gone. It was the war. He had hated it; but it had receded him from him with the suddenness of a tide sucked out by undertow, seeming to draw with it Margaret, Lucius, Lee, leaving him stranded here. It had been the medium in which his happiness with Margaret had existed. Its end marked her final loss.

It was in any case no night to be alone: it was a ritual night, a ceremonial night, marking a bloody fulfillment. He decided to go to the Leamingtons'; at eleven, the party probably was just getting into its swing. He put cold water on his face, changed his clothes and went down to the street and got into his car, realizing with a mild pleasant shock that he didn't have to worry about conserving gasoline. The streets in this part of the city were quiet; here and there noisy hilarious knots of people moved in or out of buildings, but they seemed, compared with the crowds downtown, as harmless as revelers on Halloween, mild heirs of ancient deadly rites.

As he drove a sense of peace - of course, that was exactly it, a sense of peace—began to rise within him like a gentle tide, lapping through him. A massive pressure, compounded of wartime restrictions, discomforts, the narrowing of life, a sense of grayness, a miserable consciousness of the suffering of others, guilt because he was not in uniform—all this had been lifted from him. He felt as mild, relaxed, competent and immortal as a convalescent on the first day on which he feels really well and goes downtown and says hello to his friends with a slight feeling of superiority: a man who has come through something.

From this gentle night he walked into the Leamingtons' party, which was in the early stages of frenzy. If, just at the moment Edwards came in, you could have turned that party to stone it would have made a marvelous frieze—the revels of victory—for the triumphal arch of Eisenhower Africanus or Patton Gallicus or MacArthur Asiaticus, Edwards might have been able to slip into the mood if he had arrived cold sober. But he was still logily engaged in throwing off the effects of the liquor he'd drunk earlier; he wasn't really ready yet to start drinking again. Continuing to sober up as everybody else became drunker, he was going against the grain of the party; he was very conscious of going against the grain of the party, and it made him sullen.

The Duration

Sally Leamington, big, fair, beaming with triumph and self-assurance as if the White House had called that afternoon to tell her that seven Japanese generals had been assigned to her to work as houseboys without pay—the Leamingtons' huge and rather ancient apartment had been a great trial in wartime to Sally, with all the servants off working in shipyards—Sally brought a girl over to Edwards and introduced them. It was plainly meant to be a significant meeting; and plainly the girl was miffed that he had shown up so late: she couldn't help feeling that he ought to have sensed that she would be there. But she quickly saw that he was ready to be sulky enough for two; she became humble and placating and eager to please, filling his glass for him and bringing it to him where he sat slumped in an armchair by a big window, studying the darkness with the concentration of Columbus' lookout: to see the first light gives the all-night drinker (time had passed and Edwards had reversed his trend and was beginning to feel his drinks) the sense of having taken part in an adventure.

This girl, dark and not bad-looking, reminded him of Elizabeth—he could see that she was difficult in some way. Probably that was why the Leamingtons had picked her for him—mating the rejects, he thought sourly. He gave her no encouragement and some cryptic remarks. After he had asked if her father had been in the IRA (he was thinking of Elizabeth's father) she went over to the other side of the room and spoke heatedly to Tom Leamington. Presently she attached herself to another man. Edwards sat by himself and drank; after a while he became lustful and wished he hadn't been so short with the girl. He ambled over to her, glass held loosely in his hand—he was getting quite drunk—and in slurred sentences tried to ingratiate himself with her.

The Duration

But she paid no attention and soon rather noisily left with the other man, not looking in Edwards' direction as determinedly as if he were a point of the compass, which was suspected of having given directions to the Japanese fleet.

He was one of the last at the party. Sally cooked breakfast, around four o'clock. Everybody was patient and considerate with Edwards, urging food on him but not being too pointed about it. As soon as he had left the party he became hungry — perhaps he felt a need to disparage the Leamingtons' hospitality. He drove, slowly and rather uncertainly, to an Italian restaurant in the Marina that stayed open all night. He ordered ravioli, daring the counterman to make something of it; but the counterman, who at this hour was also the cook, performing on a huge range beneath a giant copper hood, took the untimely order in his stride.

As he put the ravioli before Edwards he said: "Great it's over, huh?"

"Oh, I don't know," said Edwards, still truculent with liquor. "It had its points."

The counterman — a romantic, even though you could see when he turned to his cooking that the back of his white garb bore the motto, in invisible ink: You Get All Kinds — stared at Edwards with interest and respect. Plainly he thought Edwards was a berserker, already missing his daily portion of slaughter. Edwards ate his ravioli, drank his coffee and left a large tip. "So long, major," the counterman said.

Edwards drove down to the bay, and parked by the Marina green, a long strip of lawn bordering the water. The day was coming. The beam from the lighthouse on Alcatraz still flashing iteratively, had suffered a great drop in significance like a nightlight in a nursery, still burning at daybreak after having been left on all night

[194]

to keep spooks away, or a light over a doorway, posted as sentry by parents for a girl who doesn't get home until dawn.

As the daylight grew it drained from the bay that sense of its being a living thing that every large body of water gives off at night. Across the bay, the hills of Marin County, with Mt. Tamalpais rising behind them, seemed to huddle blackly together; they would regain their identities, seem to move apart a little as the light increased.

In the very early light the great span across the Golden Gate had the mysterious look of all large structures seen against a night sky, as if the firm which won the construction contract had secretly sub-contracted it to the builders of Stonehenge; with more light, the bridge's red-orange color became visible, giving it the appearance of a sunrise at the wrong end of the sky, in the west.

Edwards fell asleep. He was wakened by a presence. While he slept three light cruisers had passed through the Golden Gate and now, nose to tail, were heading up the bay. Their dark gray paint looked black in the early light; this, with their speed and intensity of purpose, gave them a sinister look. No one was visible on their decks; they seemed unaware that the war was over; they might have been Japanese warships, bent on striking a last blow at the enemy's city.

The sun was rising now over the Oakland hills, behind him, the stir of a normal day beginning in the city could be heard, - automobile engines, the overhead doors of apartment garages being banged up: the urban equivalents of dogs' and chickens' noises; reality seemed to be reasserting itself after the odd, strained and rather dreamlike atmosphere of his long night. He realized that the morning's normalcy was double: it was the first morning of peace. He felt flowing through him, at the thought of the war's end, a sensation of content which was even deeper than it had been last night; it was like waking up after a wedding night to the thought that these pleasures are assured and extend indefinitely into the foreseeable future.

He got out of his car, a middle-aged, and battered convertible, and, moving rather clumsily, put down its top. He drove across the bridge and into the Marin hills through the Waldo tunnel, then turned around and came back. Coming back, there is a great view of the city on its hills, before you go into the tunnel; then the tunnel's dark length; then you flash out into the light, and there is the view again. The city assumes the compact and fabulous quality of a city photographed through a telescopic lens. Salvador Dali, in a great burst of perception, painted it as a sorcerer's castle, springing from the waves mounted on a column of huge bones — dinosaur's bones, they must be.

[TWELVE]

On the other side of the continent, Margaret was washing breakfast dishes. Yesterday's newspaper, its headlines huge, lay on the floor, soon to be devoted to some domestic purpose such as wrapping up the garbage. Victory, war; she walked over the words, and the faces of statesmen, as she did her chores, contemplating a world without ration books.

The phone rang; it would be Harry, she knew almost nobody in Norfolk. Many mornings, more or less like this lay ahead of her—though on a grander scale; there would be someone to wash the dishes and answer the telephone for her. When the phone rang, how often would it be Harry? Should she, sometimes, eagerly hear another voice, one which she didn't now know? But these questions hadn't yet occurred to her.

*   *   *   *   *

On the return trip the man at the toll gate gave Edwards a shrewd but good-humored look of assessment. No doubt he looked pretty beat up: but this was a morning when much could be understood and tolerated, the toll gate guard's smile said.

Back in the city, he turned off Marina Boulevard onto Fillmore Street. A pretty girl, neatly packaged except for a yawn, was waiting at a bus stop. She snapped short the yawn and smiled at him boldly. He would have stopped and offered her a lift, but he felt too unshaved and unkempt. Anyway, this was a day of arrival, not of departures. He had a sense of rocking gently at anchor, like a craft come into port. An anchor implies the probability, the almost certainty of more voyages. On the first day after a great war Edwards, as any sensible man who abhors destruction should, thought about love and the pleasures of the flesh. He thought that women lay ahead of him, undiscovered, like tropical islands: islands filled with beautiful women; for it's true after you pass a certain point, in years or experience, that your later women are inhabited by your earlier women. The cannon you fire as you enter the harbor of a new love, makes echoes.

[GLOSSARY]

1. **mahouts** — elephant drivers in India
2. **Tanforan** — a race track that operated in San Bruno, California, from 1899-1964; the track makes an appearance in the 2003 movie *Seabiscuit*
3. **tumuli** — artificial mounds of debris such as those found at archaeological sites
8. **wraith had presided over Nepenthe** — a wraith is an apparition or spirit often said to appear to portend one's death; Nepenthe is a drug, often cited in mythology to cure depression
   Assyrian methods — the Assyrians, a people of Mesopotamia, several centuries BC, were noted for their cruel tortures
   Louis XV on the mistakes of Louis XIV - kings of France, members of the **Bourbon** dynasty — the royal house of France and Spain
9. **Attila's** — Atilla the Hun, who conquered much of Eastern Europe in the 5TH century
   Sans Soucis — French for "without worries" often used as a name for places of retreat, such as a Haitian king's palace
   Levant — the Mediterranean region of the Middle East
10. **Charles V** — according to legend, the Holy Roman Emperor's funeral was held prematurely and he allegedly

rose out of the coffin in the middle of the ceremony

obituary not only wasn't written — newspapers constantly update obituaries to always have them ready to go in case someone famous dies

DAR - Daughters of the American Revolution, an aristocratic group formed by old families

13. **Alexander's sword through the knot** — according to legend, Alexander the Great solved the problem of how to undo the Gordian knot by cutting it

16. **Front de Boeuf** — a character in the novel Ivanhoe, a ruthless knight with a scarred, intimidating face

17. **4-F** — a draft classification designating someone as unfit for military service due to a medical condition

18. **N.Bonaparte, passage booked at Elba** — Napoleon Bonaparte was exiled to the island of Elba after his forced abdication in 1814

    Roger Casement — (1864-1916) an Irish revolutionary, noted for investigating human rights abuses around the world; executed by the British government

20. **hundred years** — The Hundred Years War 1337-1435. Because men drafted into World War II were drafted "for the duration" there was concern as to how long the war would last

    Parkinson's Law — the idea proposed by Cyril Parkinson that work expands to fill the time allotted for its completion. This reference is anachronistic in that the first recorded reference of Parkinson's law was not until 1955, 10 years after the war

    stamps — ration stamps were required to purchase scarce commodities like meat

23. **leg makeup** — Nylon was scarce during the war so women painted their legs, including drawing in a seam to make it look as though they were wearing stockings

24. **"C" windshield sticker and ration book** — Cars had stickers designating how much gas they were entitled to, but ration stamps were still required to purchase gas and tires

    frozen — to prevent inflation, wages and prices were frozen during the war

35. **Penelope** — the wife of Odysseus, who patiently waited for

The Duration

his return from the Trojan War, while keeping suitors at
bay

**Macedonians at those difficult dinner parties Alexander
used to give for the Persians** — Alexander the great was
known to hold executions at the end of dinners, lopping off
the heads of some guests

36. **Andromea have paid to Perseus** — Perseus is a hero of
Greek mythology who recued Andromeda from a sea
monster

38. **Gibsons** — a drink popular at the time, made of gin and vermouth and traditionally garnished with a pickled pearl
onion

40. **Ludlow Fair** — an event in ancient England, renowned for
being a good time, referred to in an A.E.Houseman poem

41. **Gerald Kersh** — (1911-1968) British writer, known for his
stories of London's underworld

Lionel, Lord Tennyson — (1889-1951), the 3rd Lord
Tennyson, famed cricketer and hero of World War I, the
grandson of the poet, Alfred, Lord Tennyson

Lawrence Tibbett — (1896-1960) American opera singer

William Saroyan's — (1908-1981) Saroyan was an American
writer, born in Fresno and raised in Oakland, California

43. **Ottoman Empire** — centered in what is now Turkey, it was
one of the largest and longest-lasting empires in history
1299-1923

44. **family physician to Philoctetes** — Philoctetes was wounded in the Trojan War, his wound festered, and the doctor
was exiled as punishment for failing to heal the hero

46. **jacquerie** — the revolt of the peasants in France in 1358

47. **vagabond's singing to hell with Burgundy** — reference to a
song in the popular operetta of the 1920's, *The Vagabond
King* by Rudolph Friml

Father Hopkins' nun — a reference to a poem "Heaven-
Haven" by Gerard Manley Hopkins (1844-1889) that com-
pares a nun entering a convent to a ship seeking a harbor
to be safe from a storm

48. **Roland** — an eighth century European hero, immortalized
most notably in the eleventh century poem, *The Song of
Roland*

50. **Rooseveltian...Hyde Park** — Franklin Roosevelt was from Hyde Park, NY
51. **cosset** — to pamper, as a pet
52. **Lucillus... Lucius Licinius Lucillus** — (circa 117 BC — circa 57 BC), a Roman politician noted for spending his war booty on public works

    William S.Hart — a star of early western movies
54. **Boccaccio and his friends safely out of a city full of the plague-stricken** — Giovanni Boccaccio's (1313-1375) famous novel, the Decameron, takes place during the plague and some scholars believe it was based on his actual experiences escaping the Black Death in Florence when an outbreak there killed seventy-five percent of the population

    slivovitz — an alcoholic beverage made from plums; sometimes called "plum brandy"
55. **Hollywood bed** — a mattress on a metal frame, often designed for easy storage. "Hollywood" was a brand name for these beds that were popular in the 1920s
58. **Stuart stubbornness maintained across the water their Pretensions** — the Stuart family, at various time in the seventeenth and eighteenth century although living in exile abroad, never gave up their claims to the British throne
59. **"MacArthur le Magnifique, A Tombé sur une Autre Ile,"** —French for "To MacArthur, the magnificent, falls another island"
60. **Colin Kelly** — the first American hero of World War II, shot down while attacking a Japanese carrier with bombs shortly after Pearl Harbor
64. **Lysistrata** — a play by Aristophanes in ancient Greece about women refusing to have sex with their husbands for political reasons
65. **droit de seigneur** — the supposed right of a lord to have the "first night" with a new bride
71. **Hook watched Peter** — Captain Hook and Peter Pan in J.M. Barrie's story
72. **Talleyrand's** — Charles Maurice de Talleyrand-Perigord (1754- 1838) French diplomat and contemporary of Napoleon, who through skill or cunning managed to

always come out on top regardless of who was in power during numerous upheavals

78. **Farragut** — Admiral David Farragut (1801-1870) was a naval hero of the Civil War, established the Navy Yard at Mare Island, San Francisco 1854-1858

79. **Sophocles and Marx and Freud and St.Augustine and Joyce** — Sophocles, a ancient Greek playwright known for the quintessential plays of complicated parent-child relationships (*Oedipus* and *Electra*); Karl Marx, the "father of communism and noted for his comments on society; Sigmund Freud, the father of psychoanalysis; St. Augustine, Catholic philosopher, known for his firm views on various points of theology, including original sin; James Joyce, Irish writer, known for books depicting often dysfunctional families

81. **Stanleys at Bosworth Field** — Lord Thomas Stanley and Sir William Stanley commanded a large private army and at the Battle of Bosworth field in 1485, held their troops aside until they knew which side was winning then committed to helping the victorious side

    Coevals — of the same age or period

    Atreide conflicts — a reference to ancient Greek myths about the descendents of Atreus, which, depending on the version of the myth, may include incest and the cooking and eating by Thyestes of his own sons

85. **Hieronymous Bosch** — (1450-1516) Dutch painter, known for his scenes of fantasies, often with many wild scenes packed into one painting

85-86. **Babylonian; but the message Belshazzar** — Belshazzar is ascribed by myth to have been king of ancient Babylon

86. **Rommel** — Erwin Rommel, (1891-1944) German Field Marshall, Commander of the Afrika Korps

87. **"Twelfth Naval District Commando"** a sarcastic term applied to men who worked in offices in a naval command instead of going overseas. Similar terms such as "Culver City Commandos" were used for movie stars who made movies instead of volunteering for combat

    Jan van Eyck — (circa 1395-1441) Dutch painter, known for his depictions of women who were possibly pregnant

manhattans — a drink popular at the time made with whiskey and vermouth

Scarlett O'Hara — the main character of the novel *Gone With the Wind*, which was made into a movie in 1939

88. **Kensington Gardens** — the gardens in London surrounding Kennsignton Palace, a royal residence

Dr. Johnson — Samuel Johnson (1709-1984) British writer and essayist, known for his clever sayings

92. **Eliza Doolittle** — a main character in George Bernard Shaw's play *Pygmalion*, and the musical based on it, *My Fair Lady*; she is a an uneducated child of the street who is taught the manners to be passed off as a duchess

Normans — the descendents of Norse Vikings who settled in Normandy in northern France and launched numerous attacks on the British Isles

Venus of Melos — also known as the Venus de Milo, a statue thought by some to embody perfect beauty

93. **sonny in the song** — a reference to a song made famous by Al Jolson, "I want a Girl Just Like the Girl that Married Dear Old Dad"

IRA in the Time of Troubles — the Irish Republican Army, during the fight for Irish independence 1912-1922

96. **Theodora** — (circa 500-548), wife of Byzantine Emperor Justinian I, she was a saint of the Orthodox Church

99. **Lord Acton** — (1834-1902) John Dalberg-Acton, British Baron, most known for his oft-quoted assertion: "Power tends to corrupt, and absolute power corrupts absolutely."

104. **Zulu impis** — Zulu troops famed for their fierceness in battle and unswerving allegiance to their commanders

109. **Promehteus'-** in Greek mythology, he steals fire from the gods and gives it to men; as punishment he is chained to a rock and has his liver eaten every day by a great bird, only to his liver grow back that night to repeat the process the next day

110. **Gogol, not Dostoevsky** — Russian writers. Nikolai Gogol (1809-1852) was known for his romantic works and Fyodor Dostoevsky (1821-1881) was known for his troubling stories and tormented characters

113. **Griselda** — a figure made legendary for her patience; char-

acters named Griselda and based on this theme appear in stories by Boccaccio and Chaucer and others

116. **Pygmalion, who may sometimes have regretted he hadn't left Galatea marble** — in Ovid's story from ancient Rome, Pygmalion is a sculptor who falls in love with his statue carved from Galatea marble; with the help of the gods it comes to life

   Macbeth to plead with Macduff — in a key scene in Shakespeare's play, Macbeth pleads with Macduff, not wanting to kill him

118. **Caesar's wife** — the model of virtue, supposedly beyond reproach and suspicion

119. **John Silver** — the fictional pirate from Robert Louis Stevenson's "Treasure Island"

   Henry Morgan - (circa 1635-1688) British pirate

126. **Nelson** — Viscount Horatio Nelson (1758-1805) British naval hero who had lost the sight of an eye in battle

   Jolly Roger — the traditional pirate flag emblazoned with skull and crossbones

127. **Berserker** — a Norse warrior who flew into a frenzy in battle; by extension, anyone who revels in war

128. **Jacobite king** — the claimants to the British throne from the Stuart family, often living in exile while attempting to have their crowns restored

129. **Walter Lippmann** — (1889-1974) noted writer and political commentator

   encomiums — formal expressions of praise, such as eulogies

130. **Rosalind — disguised-as-a-young-man** — a character from Shakespeare's "As You Like It" who dresses up as the young man Ganymede

   Annie Oakley — (1860-1926) sharpshooter and star of wild west shows

130. **Desdemona's...for Othello** — in Shakespeare's play "Othello," Desdemona is married to Othello and while appearing to be mild, is actually quite determined and forceful

131. **Buchenwald** — a German concentration camp

132. **dynamited when the Fire** — after the great San Francisco earthquake in 1906, firebreaks were dynamited to stop the

The Duration

fire from spreading, sacrificing whole streets of houses to save the rest of the city

134. **Goebbels-like** — Joseph Goebbels, Ph.D., was Minister of Propaganda for the Third Reich, noted for verbal gymnastics to make try to spin the crimes of Nazi Germany in a positive way

135. *Vestris* — a famous shipwreck; in 1928 it went down off the coast of Virginia taking over 100 people to their deaths
General Slocum — a New York City excursion boat that caught fire and sank in 1904, killing 1,021 of the 1,342 people on board in one of the worst maritime disasters in history

136. **divagations** — wanderings, strayings

138. **chicken Raphael Weill** — Weill was an early merchant in San Francisco who liked to cook. His recipe for chicken is still served in Bay Area restaurants.

142. **breadfruit** — the cargo the Bounty was carrying when the mutiny occurred; often used as a symbol of paradise
Melville's catalog of whiteness — in his novel, "Moby Dick," Herman Melville has a long list of white things, comparing them to the color of the whale

145. **Keystone Cops...for cross-eyed Turpin** — a series of silent films starred slapstick police in the distinctive uniforms of that era; one of the stars was a cross-eyed actor, Ben Turpin

147. **interregnum** — the gap in time between rulers, or any formal break in continuity
M.F.H's — Master of foxhounds. One who oversees a hunt and takes care of the dogs

150. **star shell** — a missile exploded over a battlefield to light it up at night

153. **appurtenances** — accessories

154. **General Romulo** — Carlos Romulo (1899-1985) was a Filipino general on the staff of Douglas MacArthur during World War II

157. **Arthur's people...arms of Arthur's sister** — King Arthur was, at least according to legend, an early king of Britain; in some versions of the tale, Arthur is seduced into unknowingly sleeping with his sister, Morgan, who then gives birth to the evil Mordred

168. **Missimo** — (1898-2003) the nickname of Soong May-Ling, the wife of Generalissimo Chiang Kai-shek, commander of the nationalist forces in China during and after World War II

    Averell Harriman — W.Averell Harriman (1891-1986) U.S diplomat during World War II

    Wendell Wilkie — ran as a Republican for president in 1940, was resoundingly defeated by Franklin Roosevelt; Wilkie died in 1944

170. **Ivan the Terrible** — (1530-1584) Tsar of Russia; as the name implies, he was known for his brutality

171. **Hoyle** — Edmund Hoyle, known for compiling and recording the rules of games; "according to Hoyle" came to mean "by the official rules" of anything

    Oedipus and Jocasta — there is great sarcasm in the "as simple" as their relationship; Oedipus is Jocasta's son and later her husband in the twisted tale by Sophocles

172. **Borgia** - a ruthless family of Italian aristocrats and popes of the fifteenth and sixteenth centuries, known for among other things, poisoning guests

173. **WCTU** — Women's Christian Temperance Union, it pushed for Prohibition and was opposed to all alcohol, even altar wine in religious ceremonies

    James Joyce — (1882-1941) known for great descriptions of interesting characters

    Nelson Algren — (1909-1981) American writer known for his shady underworld characters

    John L.Sullivan — (1858-1918) Heavyweight boxing champion

    Niall of the Nine Hostages — an Irish King of the fourth and fifth centuries, like Arthur, as much myth as real

    Pimm's Cup — a fruity alcoholic drink made in Britain, often served as a liqueur

177. **Mme.Defarge than with the Vicomtesse de Beauharnais** — Defarge is the villain of Charles Dickens' "Tale of Two Cities," working on the side of peasants in the French Revolution; Beauharnais was the wife of Napoleon and empress of France

178. **Botticelli's girl** — the Italian painter's famous painting, *The*

Birth of Venus, shows the goddess emerging naked from
the sea

179. *Quelle ronde* — a French idiom for *"what a world"*

181. **trepanned** — trepanning is surgery in which a hole is drilled
in the skull

183. **Saturnalia** — a winter solstice celebration in ancient Rome

184. **Aix** — a town in France, the scene of a battle in 102 BC that
was followed by the mass suicides of the town's women

185. **mandarin** — used here, it is used as a synonym for a
Chinese person

186. **souped** — to put film into the "soup" of chemicals to develop photographs

190. **Cossacks in Petrograd of 1917** — during the Russian
Revolution, the Cossacks, charged with defending the
Winter Palace, instead defended the protestors against the
police

knouts — whips used in Russia for beating criminals

**tear gas, bombs, gunfire, strewn bodies, grim silent
marchers, on a day in 1934** — riots along Market Street and
the police reaction during a general strike left several dead

bacchantes — the followers of Bacchus, the Roman god of
wine, and by extension, drinking and partying

Richard Taylor grew up in San Francisco in the 1920s and 30s. Although he was a young man during WWII, like his fictional protagonist in *The Duration*, he was 4-F, so did not serve in the military. He was a gifted student who graduated from Stanford; while a student there he was part of a longitudinal study of students with extremely high I.Q.s that followed their careers over a 30 year period. He was a journalist, writer, and an editor during his entire professional life. The last publications he edited were *The Valley News* in El Cajon, CA and the *Labor Leader* in San Diego. He was also a correspondent for the *Los Angeles Times* and had articles published in *San Diego Magazine* as well as a history of the Lakeside-Santee area for the County of San Diego. As a history buff, Richard could have been a brilliant college history professor but thought college teaching was too political. He could talk for hours about battles that most of the population had never heard of. The Battle of Stanford Bridge in 1066, just 13 days before the Battle of Hastings, was one of his favorites. He had read every word he could find on it and would quote things reportedly said by Harold of Norway the day prior to the battle as if they had been said the day before he stated his own eloquent recollections. He was equally adept at quoting the generals of the American Civil War and wrote another novel set during that war—a brilliant and well-researched work, it was never published and unfortunately, the only copy of that manuscript was lost. He was also a Kennedy scholar and admirer and listened to recordings of JFK's speeches when time allowed.

The Duration

Richard was married to my mother, Jean, from 1963 to 1978. He was a fashionable dresser and like his mother had an affinity for San Francisco culture even though he lived on a ranch in Lakeside near San Diego. He had a daughter, Lynn, from a previous marriage. He was a wordsmith and editor par excellence. He delighted in reading and editing my writing as well as the writing of my students. He passed away in 1979 and left this manuscript to my mother who left it to me when she passed away in 2009. I and Walt Meyer present *The Duration* to you in Richard's memory.

Mark Hanson, Ph.D., San Diego, 2012